Young Love

"You what?" Clint asked as they left the building.

"I love Lola."

"No, you don't," Clint said. "You love what she has between her legs."

"That's what she said."

"Well, she's right," Clint said, "and so am I. Come on, we have some riding to do."

"Riding?" Roscoe asked. "Ain't we gonna stay in a hotel?"

"Look around you, Bookbinder," Clint said. "There is no hotel here."

"So we gotta sleep on the ground again?"

"That's right. And you're going to have the first watch."

"B-but . . . I'm exhausted."

"Yeah," Clint said, smiling, "I'm sure you are."

THE TWO-GUN KID

J. R. ROBERTS

J

JOVE BOOKS, NEW YORK

THE BERKLEY PUBLISHING GROUP
Published by the Penguin Group
Penguin Group (USA) Inc.
375 Hudson Street, New York, New York 10014, USA
Penguin Group (Canada), 90 Eglinton Avenue East, Suite 700, Toronto, Ontario M4P 2Y3, Canada
(a division of Pearson Penguin Canada Inc.)
Penguin Books Ltd., 80 Strand, London WC2R 0RL, England
Penguin Group Ireland, 25 St. Stephen's Green, Dublin 2, Ireland (a division of Penguin Books Ltd.)
Penguin Group (Australia), 250 Camberwell Road, Camberwell, Victoria 3124, Australia
(a division of Pearson Australia Group Pty. Ltd.)
Penguin Books India Pvt. Ltd., 11 Community Centre, Panchsheel Park, New Delhi—110 017, India
Penguin Group (NZ), 67 Apollo Drive, Rosedale, North Shore 0632, New Zealand
(a division of Pearson New Zealand Ltd.)
Penguin Books (South Africa) (Pty.) Ltd., 24 Sturdee Avenue, Rosebank, Johannesburg 2196,
South Africa

Penguin Books Ltd., Registered Offices: 80 Strand, London WC2R 0RL, England

This is a work of fiction. Names, characters, places, and incidents either are the product of the author's imagination or are used fictitiously, and any resemblance to actual persons, living or dead, business establishments, events, or locales is entirely coincidental.

THE TWO-GUN KID

A Jove Book / published by arrangement with the author

PRINTING HISTORY
Jove edition / February 2009

ISBN: 978-0-515-14586-1

JOVE®
Jove Books are published by The Berkley Publishing Group,
a division of Penguin Group (USA) Inc.,
375 Hudson Street, New York, New York 10014.
JOVE® is a registered trademark of Penguin Group (USA) Inc.
The "J" design is a trademark of Penguin Group (USA) Inc.

PRINTED IN THE UNITED STATES OF AMERICA

10   9   8   7   6   5   4   3   2   1

ONE

When Clint entered the Hard Ace Saloon, business was good. So good, in fact, that hardly anyone paid attention to him as he walked to the bar. He attracted a little attention when he elbowed himself a space, but after getting a look at his face, the men on either side of him made room. They knew he was not in the mood to be trifled with.

There were two bartenders working the busy bar, half a dozen saloon girls working the floor, and enough patrons in the place that some were waiting in line for a turn at the blackjack, faro, and roulette tables. Up on stage several girls were singing, dancing, and swishing their skirts to the music supplied by a piano player in the corner.

Yet, among all this turmoil, Clint was able to easily pick out the table of men he was concerned with. There were five of them, but that didn't concern him. He fully intended to kill all five of them.

He ordered a beer and accepted it from the bartender with a curt nod. The man was too busy to try any small talk, but Clint would not have responded to it anyway.

He turned his back to the bar, leaned on it, and nursed his beer while he watched the five men drink, laugh, grope the girls, and slap each other on the back. They were having a grand old time, completely unaware that—possibly within minutes—they'd all be dead.

But before he killed them, he was going to make sure they knew why they were dying . . .

TWO MONTHS EARLIER . . .

When Clint rode into Evolution, Kansas, he wasn't looking to kill anyone. All he wanted was a bath, a drink, a meal, a poker game, and a bed. All in one day, if he could get it.

Evolution appeared to be in the midst of just that—change. It was a mixture of old, dilapidated, falling-down wooden structures and brand-spanking-new buildings made of both wood and brick. It was the same with the people. Some were old and worn out, others young and new—but this was the same in every town, wasn't it?

No, it wasn't. Dying towns were usually inhabited by dying people—or people who had stopped living. He could tell from the expressions on many of these people's faces that they were far from finished with living.

Today, this was a good place to be.

He dropped Eclipse off at the livery, found himself a hotel and a bath, and then made his way to the nearest saloon for a cold beer.

He entered the Silver Spur, which was in one of those brand-new buildings. Even the inside smelled new, having not yet absorbed all the booze and sweat and smoke that it eventually would.

The bartender brought him his beer and asked, "Passin' through?"

"That's right."

"Lookin' for a place to settle?" he asked. "This here town's growin' every day."

"I can see that," Clint said, "but I'm not looking for a place."

"Drifter, huh?"

"I guess you could say that," Clint said, although it wasn't the word he would have used to describe himself. But he didn't have a viable alternative at the moment, so he didn't argue.

There was no one else demanding the bartender's attention, so he started telling Clint about the new bank, the new feed store, the new school, and that brought him to the new schoolteacher.

"Now, they didn't have no schoolmarm's like this'n when I was in school, no sir."

"That a fact?"

"Yes, sir," the man went on. "Why, put a dress on her—a fancy dress, I mean—and she'd fit right in here with the saloon girls." He leaned forward and lowered his face, even though none of the saloon girls were around at the moment. "In fact, she'd put these girls to shame, she would."

"That pretty, huh?"

"Better than that," the bartender said, straightening up, "better than pretty. Fact is, a lot of the wives in town don't like her much."

"Why's that?" Clint asked, just making conversation.

"Too many of their husbands have been volunteering to walk the kids to school."

"Ah," Clint said, "I got you."

"I mean, the ladies in town usually don't like the whores in town, but hereabouts it's the schoolteacher."

"In this nice little town, huh?"

"Hey, this *is* a nice town," the bartender argued, "and it ain't so little. It's gettin' bigger by the day."

"Who's the law here?" Clint asked.

"Sheriff Greenwood."

"How long has he been wearing the badge?"

"Here? A few months. Before that I don't know. We heard he had some experience, but only the mayor and the town council know how much."

"Didn't the town vote him in?"

The bartender shrugged

"Didn't have much of a choice," he said. "Nobody else was running."

Which meant the mayor and the town council shoved Sheriff Greenwood down the town's throat.

"Politicians," Clint said.

"Yeah," the bartender said.

"Another beer, please," Clint said.

"Comin' up."

When the barman put the second beer in front of him, Clint asked, "When does the town liven up?"

"What kind of livenin' up are you lookin' for?" the man asked.

"Poker."

"Oh, after supper," the man said. "There's always a few games goin' on in here."

"Private games?"

"Open to anyone," the bartender said.

"Any house-dealt games?"

"No."

"Good."

"What's wrong with house-dealt games?"

"The house always has the edge."

"And who has the edge in a private game?"

Clint grinned and said, "I do."

TWO

Clint was on his second beer when men started drifting into the saloon looking for a drink and a card game. Some of them were looking for a drink and a girl. Still others were just looking for trouble.

"Here they come," the bartender said. "Girls'll be out in a minute. Should be a game startin' up soon enough. Want me to get you in?"

"That's okay," Clint said. "I'll watch awhile and then get myself in."

"Suit yerself."

Clint watched as chairs were pulled up to tables and decks of cards were fanned out. The girls came down from upstairs, flashing their legs from beneath their skirts, and started carrying drinks to tables. In one corner the cover was pulled off a faro table and the dealer began to set up for a night's business.

When a young man wearing two guns walked in, Clint noticed him right away. He was on the prod, looking for trouble, and he thought he could handle it with two guns. Clint knew the type. This kid was young, probably hadn't even started to shave yet.

"Hey, here comes the Two-Gun Kid," somebody at the bar said.

"Yeah, ain't he pretty?" someone else said.

The kid did look a bit girly, with his smooth skin and his new clothes.

Clint waved the bartender over.

"You know that kid?"

"Everybody knows that kid," the man said. "Thinks he's a gunfighter."

"Does he always dress like that?"

"Yup," the bartender said. "Two guns, new clothes; when he gets closer, you'll smell the toilet water."

"Why's he come in here like that?"

"Because he's always lookin' for trouble, that's why," the barman said. "He's waitin' for somebody to say somethin' so he can throw down on him."

"Has he ever?" Clint asked. "Used his guns on a man, I mean."

"He says he has."

"Anybody know for sure?"

"Him."

The boy looked around, then walked over to the bar and slammed his hand down.

"Whiskey, bartender."

As the bartender went to serve him, Clint could see what the man meant about the toilet water. The scent was almost making his eyes water.

Next to him the two men were nudging each other and laughing. Both were dressed in trail-worn clothes and wearing equally worn guns and holsters.

"Lookee there," one of them said, "the sweet thing is drinkin' whiskey."

"Maybe we should make him buy us a drink, too," the other one said.

Clint watched as the two men walked down to where the boy was watching the bartender pour him a drink. When he was done, he moved back to stand in front of Clint.

"You know those two?" Clint asked.

"Never saw them before," the bartender said. "Passin' through, like you."

"What's the boy's name?" Clint asked.

"Roscoe."

"Those two are going to push him," Clint said.

"That's what Roscoe wants," the bartender said.

"What's your name?"

"Charlie."

"Charlie, I think you might be needing the sheriff in here."

"Maybe," Charlie said, "and maybe we should see if Roscoe is full of hot air, or if he can really handle himself."

"I can tell you just by looking at him and those other two," Clint said, "they'll kill him."

"Maybe they just wanna have a little bit of fun," Charlie said. "Might do Roscoe some good."

Clint didn't think so. If Roscoe was the kind of kid Charlie was saying he was, looking for a fight, then he'd push it and force these two to kill him.

Damn, Clint thought, why don't I just mind my own business?

• • •

The two men, Zack and Lee, partners for a couple of years, approached Roscoe as he stood at the bar, nursing his whiskey.

"That ain't no way to drink whiskey, boy," Lee said. "Ya gotta down it all at once, feel the burn as it goes down."

"Here," Zack said, "we'll show ya. Barkeep, three drinks over here."

"I don't need another drink," Roscoe said, "and I don't need no lessons on how to drink."

"You need lessons on somethin'," Lee said as the bartender poured out three shots of whiskey and then scurried away.

"Like, maybe, how ta dress," Zack said.

"And what's that smell?" Lee asked, sniffing the air. "Boy, you smell like a whore."

"Looks kinda like a whore, too, don'tcha think, Lee?" Zack asked. "Looks like a whore I fucked in the ass last time we was in Wichita."

"How about it, boy?" Lee asked. "You ever been fucked in the ass?"

Roscoe pushed away from the bar with such force that the drinks on the bar spilled. He turned and faced the two men.

"You fellas come in here lookin' for a fight, ya found the right guy," he said tightly. His hands hovered over his guns, which were pearl-handled.

"Lookee here, Lee," Zack said, "the little whore's gonna shoot us with his pretty guns."

Roscoe grinned at the two men and said, "Slap leather."

That's when Clint moved . . .

THREE

Other patrons became aware of what was happening and cleared out. Nobody wanted to get hit with any flying lead, but at the same time nobody wanted to miss the action. So those who were standing at the bar moved away, while men sitting at the tables stood up and moved out of the line of fire.

Clint was the only one who moved toward the action.

"Now, hold on, boy," he said, stepping between the antagonists.

"Get outta the way, mister," Roscoe said. "These yahoos insulted me, and they're gonna pay."

"Are you sure, son?" Clint asked. "Two against one, that's not very good odds, is it?"

"I can take 'em," Roscoe said confidently.

Zack and Lee were smirking.

"Who're you, his daddy?" Lee asked.

"I don't even know the boy," Clint said, "but I know you fellas."

"We ain't never met you before," Zack said.

"I know your type, though."

"Yeah? What type is that?" Lee asked.

"The type who will face a green kid two-to-one, but will back down from somebody with experience."

"You takin' his part?" Lee asked, licking his lips.

"That's right, I'm taking his part."

"I don't need no help, mister!" Roscoe snapped.

"Just stand quiet, kid," Clint said. "We got a lot to talk about."

"Hey—"

"What about it?" Clint asked, squaring up and facing the two men. "You want to give me a try?"

Now it was Zack who licked his lips and risked a look at Lee, who was staring wide-eyed at Clint.

"We-we don't have no beef with you, mister," Zack said.

"Naw, naw," Lee said, "that's right."

"What was your beef with this kid, then?"

"Nothin'," Zack said, "nothin'. We was just . . . kiddin', is all."

"Well, I don't think he found it funny," Clint said. He considered making the two men apologize, but that might have been pushing them too far. Instead he said, "Time for you to go, then."

"Yeah, sure," Zack said, backing away. "We can drink someplace else."

"I don't think so," a voice said.

They all looked to the door, where a man had entered quietly and watched the proceedings. He was tall and broad-shouldered, with a badge on his chest.

"I think you boys should just leave town," the sheriff said.

"We didn't do noth—" Lee started, but Zack put his hand on his friend's arm to stop him.

"Sure, Sheriff," he said. "We'll move on. We don't want no trouble."

"Funny," the sheriff said, "looked to me like that's just what you *were* lookin' for."

Zack grabbed Lee's arm and tugged him toward the doors.

"Come on, Lee," he said. "Let's get outta here."

They made their way past the sheriff and out the batwing doors. At that point it seemed as if a collective breath was let loose by the crowd, who had been anticipating some action.

"You two," the sheriff said, pointing at Clint and Roscoe, "come with me."

FOUR

"Siddown, both of you," the sheriff said as they entered his office.

He went around and sat behind his desk.

"Guns on the table, please."

"Them two was askin' for it, Sheriff," Roscoe said.

"Shut up, boy, and put your guns on the desk . . . now!"

"Do what he tells you," Clint said, setting his modified Colt on the desk.

"I don't need you to tell me," Roscoe snapped. He removed both guns from his twin holsters and set them on the desk, then sat down heavily. He took off his hat and blond bangs fell over his forehead. Clint sat down and waited for the inevitable questions.

"What's you name?" the lawman asked.

"Clint Adams."

Recognition in the man's eyes.

"What's the Gunsmith doin' in Evolution?"

"Just passing through."

"And already in trouble?"

"I was trying to stop trouble," Clint said. "I asked the bartender to send for you, but apparently he wanted to see what would happen."

"What woulda happened is I woulda killed them two," Roscoe said.

"Roscoe, shut the hell up," the lawman said. "Do you even know who this man is? Did you hear me say he's the Gunsmith?"

Apparently, Roscoe had not heard that the first time—or it simply had not registered. Now he turned his head and looked at Clint, eyes wide.

"Is that who you are?"

Before Clint could reply, the sheriff answered.

"Yeah, that's who he is, and he probably saved your life." The sheriff indicated the pearl-handled revolvers on his desk. "Come on, Roscoe, tell the truth. Have you ever even fired these weapons?"

"Sure I have," Roscoe said, looking back at the sheriff. "Plenty of times."

"I'm gonna give these back to you now, Roscoe," the sheriff said, pushing the guns across the desk, "but it's against my better judgment. Take 'em and go home. If you use them tonight, I'll throw your ass in a cell and lose the key. Got it?"

"Yeah," Roscoe said, "yeah, I got it.

"Take 'em!"

Roscoe stood up, took the guns, and returned them to his holsters.

"Adams—" he started, but the sheriff interrupted him before he could get any further.

"Get out, Roscoe, before I change my mind and

decide to keep you overnight. You'd hate break-fast."

Roscoe turned, walked to the door, and left, slamming the door behind him.

Clint looked around the small, cramped office, wondering why the town hadn't yet built the lawman a new one.

"What about me?" he asked. "When can I go?"

"How long were you plannin' to stay in town, Mr. Adams?" the sheriff asked.

"I don't know," Clint said. "I just rode in today, didn't have any definite plans."

"Looks like you got here just in time," the lawman said. "That boy's been spoilin' for a fight for months. Thinks he's Wild Bill Hickok."

"He any good with those guns?"

"Oh, I guess he can hit what he aims at," Sheriff Greenwood said. "That don't mean he can stand against one man, let alone two. Those two probably woulda killed him if you hadn't stepped in. Go on, take your gun back."

Clint leaned forward, retrieved the gun, and slid it into his holster, but he didn't get up.

"What's his full name?"

"Bookbinder," the sheriff said, "Roscoe Bookbinder. Not exactly a gunfighter's name."

"I know a gunman named Books," Clint said, "but never one named Bookbinder."

"Well," Greenwood said, "at the rate he's goin', he'll get himself killed before anyone knows who he is. Do me a favor?"

"I don't have time to look after some snot-nosed kid with illusions about being a gunfighter, Sheriff."

"I didn't think you had," Greenwood said. "That ain't what I was gonna ask you."

"Oh," Clint said. "Okay, then what were you going to ask me?"

"Just a small favor," the lawman said.

"How small?" Clint asked, getting to his feet.

"However long you decide to stay in town?" the man asked. "Try not to kill anybody, huh?"

FIVE

Clint was not surprised to find Roscoe Bookbinder waiting for him outside.

"Mr. Adams, I gotta talk to you."

"About what?" Clint asked. "The best way to get yourself killed?"

"No," Roscoe said, "the best way for me *not* to get killed."

"That's easy," Clint said. "Take off those ridiculous guns, stop wearing those ridiculous clothes, and, oh yeah, take it easy on the lilac water."

Roscoe looked down at his guns, then back at Clint.

"What's ridiculous about them?"

"Well, the pearl handles, for one."

"B-but . . . they're expensive."

"What's that got to do with how a gun performs?" Clint asked.

"Well, if they're expensive, they work better . . . don't they?"

"Boy," Clint said, "the first thing you've got to learn

is that a gun performs only as good as the man who's holding it."

With that, Clint stepped down off the boardwalk and started over to the other side of the street. Roscoe hurriedly followed.

"See? I do got a lot to learn, and you can teach me," he said, moving alongside Clint.

"I'm not a teacher," Clint said.

"You're the Gunsmith," Roscoe said. "I can learn just by bein' around ya."

Clint stopped dead in his tracks, practically in the middle of the street.

"Forget that," he said. "It's not going to happen. I can't have you following me around wherever I go."

"Why not?" Roscoe asked. "Lots of men ride together, like partners."

"I ride alone," Clint said. "I don't need a partner. Now, stop following me."

Clint started walking again, heading for the saloon. He wanted a beer, and there was still time to get in a little poker before the night was over.

Behind him Roscoe Bookbinder just stood in the middle of the street, looking forlorn.

As Clint approached the bar, Charlie met him with a beer.

"Figured you could use this."

"Thanks."

"What happened to the kid?"

"He's out there, somewhere."

"Sheriff give ya a hard time?"

"No. He was just doing his job, wanted to know how long I was going to stay in town."

"You somebody famous?"

Clint didn't answer. Charlie shrugged and moved down the bar to serve others.

Clint was working on his beer when Roscoe sidled up alongside him.

"Are you back?" Clint asked. "Looking for more trouble?"

"I was lookin' for you."

"All I can do is buy you a beer, kid," Clint said. "You want one?"

"Sure."

Clint signaled to Charlie to bring another beer. The bartender did it without comment, setting a mug in front of Roscoe.

"Look," Roscoe said to Clint, "you're right. I look silly."

"Yeah, you do."

"I'll change," Roscoe said. "I'll change my clothes, and my guns—"

"One gun," Clint said. "You don't need two guns. If you can't do the job with one, the other one isn't going to help you."

"Okay, fine, one gun," Roscoe said, "and new clothes, but there's one thing I can't change."

"What's that?"

"My attitude."

Clint looked at him.

"Well, that's most likely what's going to get you killed."

"I know it," Roscoe said, "but I know me. I can't

change who I am. I need you to teach me so's I can keep myself alive."

Clint took a long look at the kid.

"You're serious, aren't you?"

"Yeah," Roscoe said, "dead serious. Without you, I'm a dead man."

Clint studied the kid a little longer, then looked into his beer mug.

"I'll think about it."

SIX

Clint found a poker game and settled in. Roscoe remained at the bar and tried to keep a low profile, which was difficult considering his brand-new duds and his pearl handles. But he kept his mouth shut, and his swagger was toned down.

Clint couldn't help himself. He liked the kid. He liked that Roscoe Bookbinder knew who he was, knew what he could change and what he could not change. A lot of people much older than he was never found that out—never came to terms with it.

He tried to concentrate on playing poker, and even though the stakes were low, he was losing hands he should have been winning. He could feel the kid's eyes on his back the whole time.

"That's it for me, gents," he said, standing up. He'd lost about fifty dollars.

"Come on back anytime," said a man named Pike—the big winner at the table, which wasn't saying much.

"Right."

He walked to the bar and stood next to Roscoe.

"You just cost me fifty dollars."

"What'd I do?"

"You're staring a hole in my back."

"I was just—"

"Where do you live?"

"On the edge of town, in a small house my pa left me when he—"

"Go home," Clint said.

"But why—"

"Go on home and I'll come by tomorrow morning to see you."

"You mean, you'll—"

"I mean I'll come by and we'll talk about it," Clint said. "That's all I'm promising for now, kid."

"Okay, okay," Roscoe said, excitedly, "but what time—"

"Don't worry," Clint said. "Just stay home and wait for me tomorrow. I'll be by."

Suddenly, Roscoe looked suspicious.

"You ain't funnin' me, are ya?" he asked. "You ain't gonna leave town tomorrow?"

"Kid," Clint said patiently, "if I say we'll talk, we'll talk. Count on it."

"Okay," Roscoe said, excited again. "Okay, Mr. Adams, I'll see you tomorrow."

Roscoe ran out of the saloon so fast Charlie came over to see what was up.

"What'd you say to him?" he asked. "I ain't never seen him move that fast."

"I just told him to go home," Clint said. "Give me one last beer before I turn in, Charlie."

"Comin' up."

While he was waiting for the beer, the sheriff came through the batwing doors before they even had time to stop swinging after Roscoe's exit.

"Saw Roscoe runnin' out of here like his ass was on fire," Greenwood said to Clint, joining him at the bar. "What happened?"

"Nothing," Clint said. "He's fine. He's just going home."

The sheriff waved to Charlie, who came over with two beers.

"Make the sheriff's beer on me, Charlie," Clint said.

"Much obliged, Adams."

They both drank down half of their beer.

"You decide what you're gonna do?" the sheriff asked.

"I might stay around a few days," Clint said. "This looks like a growing town."

"We like to think so."

"When are they going to build you a better office, and a bigger jail?"

"Believe me," Greenwood said. "I been askin' the same thing. They tell me it'll happen soon."

"Well," Clint said, "I hope it does."

"So," Greenwood asked, "what did you tell him?"

"What did I tell who?"

"Roscoe," the sheriff said. "Come on, I know the boy. He was probably waiting for you outside my office to ask you to help him. Am I right?"

Clint hesitated, then said, "Yeah, you are."

"What's he want?"

"He says without me he'll get himself killed."

"He's probably right," Greenwood said. "He just naturally rubs people the wrong way. He needs somebody to show him the way."

"The way?" Clint asked. "What the hell do I know about his way? He wants me to teach him how to be a gunfighter."

"And will you?"

"I don't know what I'm going to do, Sheriff," Clint said. "I like that the boy knows he needs help, but I don't like what he thinks he needs help for."

"So what are you gonna do?"

"If I do anything, I'll teach him how to stay alive," Clint said. "It'll be up to him for the lesson to stick."

"Well, see what you can do about those pearl-handled revolvers, will ya?"

Clint grinned and said, "That would be first on my list."

SEVEN

Clint woke the next morning with a warm, naked hip pressed to his. He didn't move. Whoever she was, he didn't want to wake her until he could remember her name and how she'd gotten there.

After the sheriff had left the saloon, Clint didn't go back to the poker game. He remembered that much. He thought he remembered having another beer— yeah, he did, he had another beer, and then a girl came over to him. One of the saloon girls.

"You coulda beat those jaspers out of all their money easy," she'd said.

"I could have?"

"Sure."

He'd turned and looked at her. Blond, tall, long legs, small breasts, but hard and round. The way her dress cupped them made that obvious.

"How do you know?"

"I know poker."

"You do, huh?"

"Yeah, I do."

"Then why didn't I win?"

"You were . . . distracted."

"You noticed that, huh?"

"I watch people," she said. "It's what I do to keep from going crazy here."

The conversation was coming back to him now. He kept replaying it in his head, hoping to come to her name.

"How do you decide who to watch?"

"I watch people I think are interesting," she said. "I noticed you as soon as I came downstairs."

"Oh? Why?"

"Because other people were watching you," she said. "They recognized you as . . . someone."

"You tell me your name," he'd said to her, "and I'll tell you mine . . ."

"Laurie," he said, out loud.

She stirred next to him, pressed her hip more tightly against his. Then she rolled so that it was her taut ass that was pressing against him.

"Good morning," she said.

The smell of her, and feel of her, had his cock hardening already as he turned to face her. He pressed the length of himself along the cleft between her butt cheeks and grew harder still.

"Oh!" she said brightly, rubbing her butt against him. "I can see it *is* going to be a good morning."

He remembered now that they had rushed back to his room when she got off work and the saloon closed. Hurriedly, they had removed each other's clothes and dived onto the bed together.

But he had no time to play that encounter back. Laurie parted her legs now so he could slide his penis up between her thighs and into her vagina, which was wet and waiting. She sighed and leaned back against him as he started to move inside of her. He reached around to caress her breasts and nipples at the same time.

"Oh, yeah," she moaned, "this is the way to wake up in the morning."

He nuzzled her neck and said, "I couldn't agree more."

"And you remember my name," she said, tossing her head back and laughing. He cut her off by kissing her, her tongue darting avidly into his mouth.

After several minutes she began to breathe harder. She pulled away from him, so that he slid from her wetly; then she quickly turned around, pushed him on his back, and mounted him.

"You did all the work last night," she reminded him. Did he? "Just lie back and relax."

She began to ride him. He relaxed and enjoyed it for a while, but eventually he had to take a more active part. He reached for her firm breasts, popped the nipples between his fingers, then pulled her down onto him so he could lick and bite them. Her breath began to come more harshly. She pressed her hands to his chest, leaned all her weight there while continuing to bounce up and down on him. Suddenly, he felt her tremble, and then she was overcome by an orgasm. But that didn't stop her. She continued to hop and ride and corkscrew on him, enjoying climax after climax until finally she collapsed onto him, exhausted.

But he wasn't done.

He rolled her off of him onto her back, straddled her, and drove himself into her. She wrapped her legs around him as he drove himself into her again and again, faster and faster, until finally he found his own climax and exploded into her . . .

Clint had breakfast in the hotel dining room while Laurie continued to sleep upstairs. He told her to use the bed as long as she wanted.

After breakfast he walked through town until he reached the house Roscoe Bookbinder had described to him. It was run-down, shutters falling off the sides, a few windows broken. If he hadn't been told different, he would have assumed it had been abandoned.

He approached the front door and knocked. It was opened almost immediately.

"It's about time," Roscoe said. "I was startin' to worry that . . ."

"That what? I'd left town? I told you I wouldn't do that."

"No offense," he said, "but lots of people have told me things they didn't mean."

"Like who?" Clint asked. "Your parents?"

"I don't want to talk about them," Roscoe said. "You wanna come in?"

"Let's walk."

"Fine."

Roscoe came out, left the door ajar.

"You want to lock your house?"

"There ain't nothin' in there to steal," the boy said.

"Everythin' that means anythin' to me is right here."
He touched his two guns.

"You're still wearing those, huh?"

"I just didn't want to leave them behind," he said.
"But look, I changed my clothes."

"Yeah, you did."

The clothing was toned down, but it was still anything but plain. Fancy stitching, too many shiny
buttons—still clothes that would cause him to be made
fun of.

"You don't like 'em?"

"They're very pretty," Clint said, "but why do you
want to be teased?"

"Anybody teases me has to deal with these," Roscoe
said, again touching his guns.

"Where do you get the money for these clothes?"
Clint asked.

"I got money."

"Why don't you use it to fix your house?"

"That's not my house," he said. "It was my father's,
and I don't care if it falls down around my ears. I ain't
gonna stay there anyway."

"No? Where are you going?"

"I'm gonna hit the trail," Roscoe said, "travel
around the country."

"If you don't get yourself killed," Clint said. They
were walking toward town. "You got money on you?"

"Some. Why?"

"We're going to buy you some new clothes . . ."

EIGHT

When they came out of the general store, Roscoe was wearing his new clothes—simple trail clothes. No fancy stitching, no shiny buttons. The only thing shiny he had on was the twin pearl-handled Peacemakers in his hand-tooled double-rig holster.

"These clothes itch," he complained.

"You'll get used to it."

"I don't stand out in these."

"You'll get used to that, too." Clint looked at his feet. "We'll have to get you some new boots, too, but that can wait."

Roscoe looked down at his expensive boots, also hand-tooled and elaborately stitched.

"Not my boots."

"The boots and the clothes are the easy things to replace."

"And what're the hard things?"

"Those." Clint pointed at Roscoe's guns.

"Now, wait," Roscoe said. "I thought you said I should carry one, not two. I just thought—"

"No, no," Clint said. "If we're going to do this, you need a new gun—a plain one. One that simply . . . shoots."

"Like that one?" Roscoe indicated Clint's weapon.

"Yes, like this one."

"But I know these guns."

"That remains to be seen."

"So does all this mean you are gonna teach me?"

"Are you willing to learn?"

"Well, yeah."

"Then come on."

Clint decided to start from scratch with Roscoe, and to teach him his first lesson at the same time.

They walked together to the gunsmith shop, the kid still grumbling, wondering why he couldn't use his own guns.

"Do you want to learn?" Clint asked.

"Sure, I do, but—"

"Then you have to do things my way."

"But you said you wanted to see if I can shoot."

"I do."

"Well, I can, but with my own gun."

"If you can shoot," Clint said, "you should be able to do it with any gun."

"Well," Roscoe said, "as long as it's a decent gun . . ."

"That one?" Roscoe asked, appalled.

"Yes, that one," Clint said.

"That's a good weapon," the gunsmith said, taking it out of the display case and handing it to Clint.

"Yes, it is," Clint agreed. It was a .36-caliber Colt Navy.

"It's ancient," Roscoe complained.

"It's broken in," Clint said. "Here, try it."

He handed the gun to Roscoe, after checking to be sure it wasn't loaded. Roscoe immediately tried to pull the trigger.

"It's broken," he complained.

"It's single-action," the man behind the counter told him.

"What?"

"You have to cock the hammer back with your thumb before you can pull the trigger," Clint told him.

"What?"

"Just do it."

Roscoe cocked the hammer back, then pulled the trigger. The hammer fell with a dry click.

"How does it feel?" Clint asked.

"Heavy," Roscoe complained, "and uncomfortable."

"You'll get used to it," Clint said. He looked at the gunsmith. "How much is it?"

The man told him.

"What? For this old—" Roscoe started to complain, but Clint cut him off.

"We'll take it," he said. "Pay the man." Then he looked at the storekeeper again. "Do you have a holster?"

• • •

"Why'd we have to leave my guns with that guy?" Roscoe complained as they left the gunsmith's shop.

"Don't worry," Clint said. "He'll take good care of them."

"He wants to buy them," Roscoe said. "You heard him."

"He made you a good offer."

"I ain't sellin 'em!"

"Okay, I'm not telling you to sell them. I just didn't want to carry them around with us."

Roscoe was fiddling with the worn holster around his waist.

"Leave that alone," Clint said.

"It don't fit right."

"It fits fine," Clint said. "In fact, wear it lower. You have it too high."

"This is how I wear my gun."

"Not anymore. I don't want your elbow bent when you grab your gun. It keeps you from having a fluid motion."

While they were walking, Roscoe continued to struggle with the holster, trying to wear it lower, testing it out.

"There, doesn't that feel better when you draw it?" Clint asked.

"Well, yeah, kinda," Roscoe said reluctantly. "Where are we going?"

"Back to your house."

"What for?"

"It looked like you have a lot of room behind it," Clint said.

"There is a lot of room."

"Then that's where you're going to show me how you can shoot."

"With this?"

"With that."

NINE

The yard behind Roscoe's house was a mess, but it was what Clint wanted. There was a falling-down fence and bottles and cans littered all over. It was perfect.

"Stand there," Clint instructed Roscoe. "And leave the holster alone."

He walked around collecting bottles and cans, then set them all up on the part of the fence that was still standing—barely.

He returned to Roscoe's side and said, "Go ahead, hit something."

"What?" Roscoe asked. "Which one?"

"Right now I just want you to hit something," Clint said. "Anything."

"Draw and fire, or just fire—"

"Oh Christ, Bookbinder," Clint said, "shoot something!"

Roscoe drew his new "old" gun, rushed his shot, and didn't hit anything.

"Damn!" he shouted. "I need my guns. This gun ain't no good."

"Give it to me," Clint said. He took his own gun out of his holster, stuck it into his belt, then put the Colt Navy in its place. It was only there for a split second, though, because he immediately drew and fired. A tin can flew into the air as a result, and then he fired two more times, hitting the can with both shots, making it dance in the air before falling to the ground.

"This gun is fine," Clint said, handing it back. "Reload it."

"That was amazing," Roscoe said. "How did you fire that fast and have to cock it each time?"

"My gun used to be single-action until I modified it," Clint said, placing his own gun back into his holster.

"But . . . you hit it while it was in the air."

"All you have to do is hit it once while it's still on the fence."

Roscoe finished reloading the gun and holstered it.

"Okay, Bookbinder," Clint said. "This time just ease the gun out and shoot a tin can."

Roscoe nodded, wiped his hands on his thighs.

"I just want you to hit it once," Clint said. "Don't try to do what I did."

"Right."

He shook his hand out, then drew the Colt Navy, cocked it, aimed, and fired. A tin can flew off the fence.

"I hit it!" Roscoe exclaimed.

"You hit the fence just under it," Clint said. "I thought you said you could shoot. Why would you go looking for trouble if you can't?"

"I got a fast draw," the kid insisted. "What the hell does it matter if I can hit a tin can or not? I can get my gun out fast and get off the first shot."

"What good is the first shot if it misses?" Clint asked.

"I need my guns, Adams."

"Okay," Clint said. "Okay, we're going to go get your guns, but if you can't do any better with them, you're going to have to do it my way, okay?"

"Yeah, okay."

"Let's go."

It didn't take long to walk back to the gunsmith's shop, pick up his guns and rig, and return to the house.

"Okay, big shot," Clint said, "show me what you've got."

Roscoe turned to face the tin cans and bottles on the fence.

"No," Clint said, "face me."

"What?"

"Face me and unload your guns."

"Unload them? Why?"

"I don't want you shooting me by accident."

"What the hell—"

"Come on, Roscoe," Clint said. "I'm giving you the chance you wanted. Just unload one of them."

Roscoe took the gun from his right holster and unloaded it, then put it back.

"Okay, stand in front of me. I'm going to go first. I want you to clap your hands. Don't tell me when you're going to do it."

"Clap?"

"Yeah." Clint clapped his hands once. "Like that."

"What are you gonna do?" Roscoe asked.

"You'll see."

Roscoe stared at Clint, then clapped his hands—or tried to. Before his hands came together, Clint drew and placed his gun there. Roscoe stared at him; Clint holstered his gun.

"Try it again," he said, "faster this time."

Roscoe stared at Clint, and his eyes gave him away. Before he could clap his hands, Clint's gun was between them.

"Damn it!"

"Want to try again?" Clint asked.

"No," Roscoe said, "this time you clap. I'll show you."

"That's what I had in mind."

Roscoe readied himself in front of Clint, who quickly clapped his hands. As flesh smacked flesh, Roscoe flinched.

"I wasn't ready," he complained.

"Okay," Clint said. "You call it."

Clint put his hands at his sides and waited.

"Now!"

Clint clapped.

"I can't call it," Roscoe complained. "That warns you."

"Do it any way you want."

They tried several more times, and each time Clint clapped his hands before Roscoe could clear leather.

"Okay," Clint said, "reload."

Roscoe did.

"Any way you want," Clint said, indicating the tar-gets.

Roscoe faced the fence, then drew with both hands and fired.

TEN

Clint had to admit the boy had some speed, but speed wasn't enough. When he slowed down, he was actually able to hit something, but only using his own guns.

Clint and Roscoe went to a small café in town and had supper.

"I tell you what," he said to Roscoe. "I'll let you hang on to your own guns, but you've got to take off those pearl grips."

"Okay," Roscoe said, "okay, I can do that. Then you'll teach me?"

"Then I'll teach you."

"Why? Because I remind you of you when you were my age?" Roscoe asked.

Clint laughed.

"Bookbinder," he said, "you're nothing like me when I was your age. No, the only thing I like about you is that you were smart enough to ask for help."

"I just wanted some help, ya know, gettin' faster," Roscoe said.

"Bookbinder, you need help to stay alive," Clint said.

"Yeah, I know," Roscoe said, "my attitude."

Clint cut into his steak, speared a chunk with his fork, and paused with it halfway to his mouth.

"Where did that attitude come from anyway?" he asked.

"I dunno," Roscoe said. "I guess I just ain't never been worried about dyin'."

"Did you get that attitude before or after your parents died?"

"I don't rightly know," Roscoe said. "They been dead a long time, and I been on my own for most of it."

With no male influence, it was no wonder he'd turned out the way he had.

"So when do my lessons start?"

"They started."

"The clapping stuff? Where did you come up with that?" Roscoe asked.

"Learned it from a fellow named Chris."

"Chris what?"

"Just Chris. That's all I ever knew."

"What did he do?"

"He specialized in forming small groups to take on larger ones," Clint said.

"And you worked with him?"

"Once," Clint said.

"Why only once?"

"Believe me," Clint said, "once was enough. Men who worked with him had a habit of not coming back."

"So what're we gonna do?"

"I have a couple of ideas," Clint said. "I just have to decide which one I like best."

"What ideas?"

"I'll tell you later," Clint said.

"So we're done for the day?"

"We're done," Clint said, "except you're going to go back to that gunsmith and have him replace the grips on your guns. Right?"

"Yeah, right. And what are you gonna do?"

"I'm going to get me a chair, sit in it," Clint said, "and think."

"That's all?"

"That's all."

"Don't sound like much," Roscoe said.

"Bookbinder," Clint said, "your first lesson is an easy one. Listen, don't talk."

"But?"

"What'd I just say?"

"Listen, don't talk."

"Very good. Remember that."

After they ate, they left the café and stopped outside.

"I want you to move into the hotel," Clint said.

"Why?"

"Because that house is bound to fall down around your ears," Clint said. "I'll pay for the hotel."

"I got money," Roscoe said. "I can pay for my own hotel."

Clint liked that the boy wanted to remain independent.

"Okay," Clint said. "Pay for it yourself."

"How long do I take the room for?"

"Start with one night," Clint said. "I'll know more about what we're going to do tomorrow morning."

"Okay," Roscoe said, "then I'll just leave most of my gear at the house."

"Whatever you say," Clint said. "I'll see you in the morning."

"Where are you goin'?"

"I'll probably be in the saloon tonight," Clint told him.

"Well, I'll be there, too."

"I don't want you to go into the saloon if you're going to look for trouble, Bookbinder," Clint said. "I don't want you getting killed before I can teach you anything."

"I ain't."

"And don't change your clothes, or switch to your pearl handles."

"How can I?" Roscoe asked. "You're havin' that gunsmith replace the grips, and we didn't even pick them up yet. I gotta wear this Colt Navy until tomorrow."

"Good," Clint said, "then you won't be in such a hurry to use it."

"Well," Roscoe said, "nobody better push me, is all. I mean, I ain't gonna look for trouble, but I ain't gonna back down either."

"I'm not asking you to back down," Clint said. "Just . . . keep calm, and be careful."

"I ain't the type to keep calm if somebody's proddin' me," Roscoe pointed out.

"Bookbinder," Clint said, "that's one of the main things you're going to learn."

"To keep calm if somebody's pushin' me?"

"How to keep calm," Clint said, "period."

ELEVEN

Clint was in the saloon early, worried that Roscoe Bookbinder might get there first and immediately get himself into trouble. Laurie came over to say hello and ask if she'd see him later.

"I hope so," he said, "unless you get a better offer between now and then."

"I doubt it," she said. "Not with what this town has to offer in the way of men."

She went off to work the floor as the batwings opened and the sheriff came in. The lawman spotted Clint and walked over to join him.

"Get you a beer, Sheriff?"

"I owe you one," Greenwood said, signaling the bartender for two.

"How are things goin' with you and your student?" he asked Clint.

"Slowly."

"You get those pearl grips off his guns?"

"I did do that, yes."

"Then you made progress," Greenwood said. "I could never convince him to get rid of them."

"Any particular reason why he should listen to you?" Clint asked. "Other than the fact that you're the law?"

"Oh, I didn't tell you?" Greenwood asked. "The boy's my nephew."

Clint turned to face the lawman and said, "No, neither one of you mentioned that."

"His mother was my sister."

"Then why's he living in that run-down shack if he's got family in town?"

"I don't live much better," Greenwood said. "I got no wife, no other family. Fact is, I spend most every night in one of my cells."

"I think one of your cells would be better than where he's living now," Clint said. "I also convinced him to move into the hotel tonight."

"Why'd you do that?"

"I'm thinking about leaving town tomorrow."

"After you told him you'd teach him, you're gonna run out on him?"

"No," Clint said, "I was thinking about letting him ride with me for a while."

"Why would you do that?"

"The boy needs direction," Clint said, "and I don't particularly want to stay in this town for as long as it's going to take for me to give it to him."

"Yeah, but why that much interest in Roscoe?" Greenwood asked. "I mean, I appreciate it and all, but I'm just curious. He remind you of yourself?"

"You know, he asked me the same question," Clint said. "He's nothing at all like me."

"Then why?"

"I just don't want to see the kid get killed early," Clint said. "And with the attitude he has now, that's what going to happen."

"Well, I'm sure his mother would've appreciated it," Greenwood said.

"He doesn't talk much about his parents."

"They were killed when he was a youngster," Greenwood said. "I wasn't here then. I left this town for a long time, came back when they asked me to be sheriff. I wasn't here when my sister and her husband were killed."

"How did it happen?"

"Best I can find out," he said, "the kid is a lot like his pa was."

"Bad attitude, you mean?"

"Seems he got some fellas mad at him and they came and took it out on him and my sister."

"What happened to her?"

"She was raped, and they were both shot."

"Where was Roscoe?"

"Hidin'."

"So he saw the whole thing?"

"Nobody knows," Greenwood said. "He ain't never talked about it."

"Well," Clint said, "I guess that explains a little bit about the kid's attitude."

"I guess so," Greenwood said. "How long you figure on keepin' him with you?"

"Not long," Clint said. "I don't want to adopt him, just smarten him up a little."

"He's really not a dumb kid," the sheriff said. "He just acts like it sometimes."

"Well then, that's as long as I'll keep him with me," Clint said. "Until he stops acting dumb."

"I wish you luck," the lawman said, raising his mug. "I been tryin' to get him to stop actin' dumb ever since I got back to this town."

TWELVE

The sheriff was gone by the time Roscoe Bookbinder came walking into the saloon. Clint had intended to wait until morning before he made his decision about whether or not to take the kid with him when he left town. However, after talking with the sheriff, he'd pretty much made up his mind. Now he had to see what the kid thought of the idea.

Roscoe looked over at Clint as he entered, unsure whether or not to join him. Clint made it easy for him and waved him over.

"Want a beer?" he asked.

"Sure," Roscoe said. "Thanks."

Clint waved at the bartender for two more beers.

"I saw the sheriff comin' out of here," Roscoe said. "What'd he want?"

"Nothing," Clint said. "We just had a beer and he told me about being your uncle."

"He ain't no kin of mine," Roscoe said.

"I thought he was your mother's brother?"

"Yeah, maybe," Roscoe said, "but I ain't callin' him no kin of mine."

"Any particular reason for that?"

"Yeah," the kid said, "but that's my business, ain't it? Ain't I entitled to my own business?"

"You sure are," Clint said. "I won't ask you anything more about it."

Roscoe peered at Clint suspiciously, then nodded and said, "Much obliged."

"I do have something to ask you, though."

"What's that?" Still suspicious.

"I've decided to leave town tomorrow."

"What?" Roscoe asked. "B-but you said—you told me you'd stay—you're supposed to—"

"Hold on, hold on," Clint said. "What did I tell you about staying calm?"

"Yeah, but—"

"Will you let me finish?"

Clearly, Roscoe wanted to go on arguing, but in the end he subsided and said to Clint, "Okay, go ahead and finish."

"I was going to ask you," Clint said, "if you wanted to ride with me."

Roscoe stared at him, clearly unsure if he'd heard right.

"What?"

"You heard me," Clint said. "I'm asking you to ride with me for a while, just until we finish with your education."

"But . . . where are you going?"

"Does that matter?" Clint asked. "Do you want to stay here so badly?"

"Well, no . . ."

"I really don't know where I'm going," Clint said. "I don't often do. I'm just going to ride."

"And you want me to come with you?" Roscoe asked. "To be your partner?"

"Bookbinder," Clint said, "I don't need a partner. You'd be riding with me to learn."

"For how long?"

"As long as it takes."

"And who's gonna decide that?"

"I will," Clint said. "When I say we're done, we're done."

"And what if we're in the middle of nowhere?"

"You'll go your way and I'll go mine," Clint said. "Come on, kid, isn't this what you want? To get out on your own?"

"Well, yeah . . ."

"You want to sleep on it?" Clint asked, picking up his beer mug. "Or drink on it?"

Roscoe hesitated only a moment and then said, "What the hell. Let's drink on it!"

THIRTEEN

Hector Ramirez was standing just a few feet away from Clint Adams and Roscoe Bookbinder at the bar in the saloon when Roscoe agreed to ride with Clint. After he heard that, Hector finished his beer and left the Hard Ace Saloon. He walked to the far end of town, where there were smaller saloons, just beer and whiskey joints, with no gambling tables, and girls you had to be drunk to sleep with. Inside one of them he found the men he was looking for—Zack Foley and Lee Orton.

"Well, well," Zack said, looking up at him, "Hector's come a-callin'."

"I got information for you," Hector said.

"What's it gonna cost us?" Lee asked.

"For now," Hector said, "A *cerveza*."

"A what?" Lee asked.

"Get the man a beer, Lee."

"Oh."

Lee got up and went to the bar while Hector pulled out a chair and sat.

"Where you comin' from?" Zack asked.

"The Hard Ace."

"Was the sheriff there?"

"For a little while," Hector said. "He was talkin' to Clint Adams."

"Mr. Gunsmith," Zack said. He closed his hands into fists. "He made a fool out of me and Lee."

"Better than havin' him kill you," Hector said.

Lee came back carrying three mugs of beer, and spilled some out of one of them while putting it down in front of Zack, who switched it with his partner.

"Who's gettin' killed?" Lee asked.

"Hector's about to tell us what he heard at the Hard Ace," Zack said.

"Clint Adams is leavin' town tomorrow."

"So?" Lee asked.

"He's takin' that kid with him."

"What kid?" Lee asked.

"That duded up kid with the pearl handles, stupid," Zack said. "It was his fault the Gunsmith made fools outta us."

"We're lucky he didn't kill us," Lee said.

"Yeah, well now he's the one who's gonna get killed," Zack said. "Him and his little friend."

"The kid looks different," Hector said, sipping his beer. "He's got different clothes and no more pearl handles."

"Adams is takin' him under his wing," Zack said.

"Gonna turn the kid into a gunfighter?" Lee asked.

"Maybe," Zack said, "but that'll take time, and I don't aim to give him enough of it."

"What are we gonna do?" Lee asked.

"We're gonna kill 'em."

"Both of them?"

"Both of them."

"Ourselves? Alone?"

"Yeah, ourselves," Zack said, "and no, not alone. We'll get some help."

"Like who?" Lee asked. "Hector?"

"I can shoot," Hector said. It sounded like he said, "choot."

"Sure, Hector can help," Zack said, "but I got somebody else in mind, too."

"Who?" Lee asked.

"Yeah, who?" Hector echoed.

"You'll see," Zack said, "you'll see. Drink up, boys. We got some work to do."

FOURTEEN

Clint woke the next morning, wrapped himself in Laurie's warmth, and used her for his own pleasure because he didn't know the next time he'd be with a woman. After that he left her there and went down for breakfast with Roscoe. The kid had packed some saddlebags, and that was all. Clint had told him they were going to travel light.

"We got to pick up my guns before we go," he said.

"Okay," Clint said. "Let's get the horses first."

They went to the livery and saddled their horses. Roscoe had a useful little mustang that would never be able to run with Eclipse, Clint's Darley Arabian, but he'd be able to walk all day, and he'd handle rough terrain.

They rode to the gunsmith's shop and woke the man up. He came downstairs, opened his shop, and gave Roscoe back his guns.

Outside, Roscoe strapped the guns back on and they mounted up.

"Where we headed?" Roscoe asked.

Clint pointed and said, "That way."

Clint was right about the mustang. The animal could walk all day, as could Eclipse, but they finally had to rest for their two-legged partners.

Clint gave Roscoe a choice: see to the horses or the fire. The kid picked the fire, and had it going by the time Clint returned from turning out their mounts.

"What do we got for food?" Roscoe asked.

"I usually travel light," Clint said. "Coffee, jerky, and beans. And we'll save the beans for later, so tonight coffee and beef jerky."

Clint put the coffeepot on, then dug in his saddle-bags for the jerky and handed Roscoe a piece.

"This is all we eat?" Roscoe complained.

"For now."

Roscoe sat across the fire from Clint and took a bite. When the coffee was ready, Clint poured it out and handed a cup across to the younger man.

"Don't look into the fire," he advised. "It'll ruin your night vision."

"What's the difference?" Roscoe asked. "We ain't lookin' for nobody, and nobody's lookin' for us."

"You never know when a man or an animal is going to come out of the dark at you," Clint said, "and if you've been staring into the fire, you'll never see them."

"But what if—"

"You ask too many questions, boy."

"Well, how the hell else am I gonna learn?"

"Listen," Clint said. "Just listen to what I tell you

and stop asking questions. Everything I tell you is a lesson you need to learn."

"Fine," Roscoe said.

It was obvious that the boy had never been in a camp, but had spent his whole life in town. Clint told him he was going to have the first watch.

"Keep the fire going, keep the coffeepot full," Clint said, "keep an eye on the horses, and keep a sharp eye and ear out."

"What am I supposed to hear?"

"You might hear somebody approaching the camp," Clint said, "or the horses might tell you that something's happening."

"The horses? How are they gonna do that?"

"If they hear something—a man, or an animal— they'll react. If that happens, or if you even think you hear something, wake me up. If not, then wake me up in four hours."

"What if I'm not tired?" Roscoe asked. "Should I let you sleep?"

"No," Clint said, "whether you feel tired or not, you're going to lie down for four hours before we get going again. You may not sleep, but your body will rest. Do you have all that?"

"I got it."

"Okay, then," Clint said. "I'm going to turn in."

He rolled himself up in a blanket, put his head on his saddle, and turned onto his side. His holster was draped over the saddle and his gun was within easy reach.

"Good night," he said.

"Night."

Roscoe studied Clint's back. He was surprised that

anyone could sleep like that, on the ground, but before long he could tell from Clint's breathing that he was, indeed, asleep.

He turned and sat in front of the fire, then moved to the other side of it, so he could see Clint. One time he caught himself looking into the fire, and panicked. What if someone came out of the dark right at that moment? He'd never know it. Before long his night vision returned and he was able to see fairy clearly. He was surprised how wide the light from the campfire spread.

He walked over to check the horses every so often, patting their necks and making sure to be aware if they were agitated at all.

Back at the fire Roscoe Bookbinder found that he wished he had someone to talk to. He thought that was odd, because he had spent plenty of time alone over the years of his young life, and had never wished for someone to talk to. What was it about sitting around a campfire in the middle of nowhere that made him want to talk? he wondered.

Eventually he started to think he was hearing noises, but luckily before he woke Clint up, he realized it was his imagination. He would have been embarrassed to wake Clint up for nothing.

He did, however, decide to sit for a while with one of his guns in his hand.

He rubbed his hand over his gun, and realized he missed how the pearl handles had felt more than how they had looked. He decided right then and there that when his lessons with Clint Adams were done, he was going to go right back to those pearl handles.

FIFTEEN

Clint used the toe of his boot to wake the kid, who came out of his blanket like he'd heard a shot.

"Wha—"

"Time to get up."

Roscoe peered up at Clint. He clearly did not know where he was.

"Take a deep breath and look around, kid," Clint said. "Then come and have some coffee."

When Roscoe made it to the fire, Clint handed him a steaming cup.

"Sorry," the kid said. "I didn't know where I was for a minute."

"That's okay," Clint said.

"We headin' right out today?"

"No," Clint said. "You're going to do some shooting."

"At what?"

"Trees, rocks, whatever," Clint said. "Now that you've got your own guns back."

"They don't feel the same without the pearl handles." Roscoe complained.

"Don't start making excuses, Bookbinder."

"I ain't makin' excuses."

"We'll see . . ."

Zack, Lee, and Hector heard the shots after they broke their own camp.

"Comin' from that direction," Hector said.

"No," Lee said, "there." Pointing.

"We'll go that way," Zack said, pointing in the direction Hector had indicated.

They rode, then dismounted and walked. When they topped a rise, they got on their bellies and had a look.

"Adams has the kid practicing," Lee said.

"Good," Zack said. "He'll need it."

"Why don't we take them now?" Hector asked. "Right from here."

"No," Zack said, "we got to do it where people know we took the Gunsmith. That's why I sent them telegrams before we left town."

"Yeah, what were they about?" Lee asked.

"You'll see when we get to Ellsworth."

"What if Adams don't go to Ellsworth?"

"Then *I* will, and you two will keep followin' him—but not too close. He ain't no fool."

"He is busy bein' the teacher," Hector said. "He will not see."

"Can't be too careful," Zack said, "so we'll track them, not follow them. Come on."

They slid back a few feet, then got up and walked to their horses.

• • •

"You're doing better," Clint said. "You seem more re-laxed."

"I told you, I need my own guns."

"That may be," Clint said, "but you're going to have to be able to shoot with any gun."

"I can't hit shit with a rifle."

"Any handgun, then."

"When are we gonna work on my draw?" Roscoe asked.

"We already have," Clint said. "We adjusted how you wear your guns, and your draw got better."

"But is it fast?"

"It's fine," Clint said. "It's not how fast you can get your gun out, Bookbinder, it's how accurately you shoot."

"People are impressed by speed."

"People are impressed by you being alive," Clint said. "You can't impress anybody if you're dead."

"But—"

"And stop worrying about impressing people," Clint said. "Impress yourself."

"But I—"

"No questions," Clint said, cutting him off. "Come on, let's break camp and get moving."

Roscoe had to be shown how to break camp, espe-cially stamping the fire out completely. Then Clint made him saddle the horses. He stood by Eclipse so the gelding would not take a bite out of the kid.

"Mount up," Clint instructed.

"Which way are we headed today?"

"Same direction."

"That takes us to Ellsworth," Roscoe said. "Can we stop there for a hot meal?"

"No," Clint said. "You've spent one night in camp and already you want a hot meal? We'll make some beans tonight."

"So we ain't stoppin' in Ellsworth?"

"No," Clint said, "we're not."

"When do we stop in a town again?"

"Not for a while, Bookbinder," Clint said. "Not for a while."

SIXTEEN

Later that day Zack did stop in Ellsworth, to meet with the three men he'd sent telegrams to. They all sat down in the Bullhead Saloon.

"What's this all about?" Ken Randle asked. The other two men nodded. That was their question, too.

Zack told them what it was about, and the three men exchanged glances.

"If we wanted to try for the Gunsmith," Will Parker asked, "why would we need you?"

"Because I know where he is," Zack said.

"We could probably find him ourselves," Eric Stride commented.

"And I can get Darby Heston to go after him with us," Zack said.

"Why the hell would Heston need us?" Randle asked. "He'd go after Adams himself."

"Don't forget, Adams has the kid with him," Zack said.

"You said he's just a green kid," Parker pointed out.

"That may be," Zack admitted, "but he's bein' trained by the Gunsmith. That oughtta count for somethin'."

"He's got a point," Randle said.

"Where's Heston?" Parker asked.

"He'll be here today," Zack said.

"And how do you know where Adams is?" Stride asked.

"I've got people trackin' him," Zack said. "We know what direction he's goin'."

"You plannin' an ambush?" Randle asked.

"I'm plannin' on gettin' credit for killin' the Gunsmith," Zack said. "That means doin' it where folks can see and not from ambush."

"This personal?" Randle asked.

"It's some personal, for me," Zack said. "Adams made me and my partner look like a couple of fools. But it ain't gonna be personal for nobody else. It's just business."

"It'll be personal for Heston," Randle said. "From what I hear, he takes everythin' personal."

"Just don't rile him," Zack said. "He'd as soon kill ya as look at ya if ya rile him."

"You friends?"

"Kinda."

"What's that mean—kinda?" Stride asked.

Zack looked at him and said, "He's my cousin."

When Darby Heston entered the saloon, he looked around and spotted Zack, but walked directly to the bar.

"I'll talk to him," Zack told the others.

"You ain't talked to him about it yet?" Randle asked.

"I just asked him to meet me here," Zack said. "I told him it was important."

The other men all exchanged dubious glances.

"Relax," Zack said. "If he doesn't kill me, he'll come along."

Zack left the table and walked to the bar.

"He's crazy," Randle said.

"Probably," Stride said.

Heston had a beer in his hand as Zack approached him.

"Hey, Darby," he said.

"What are you doin' with those losers, Zack?" Heston asked. "Oh, wait, I forgot, you are a loser."

"Funny, Darby," Zack said.

Heston drank down half his beer and then said to his cousin, "Okay, get to why you asked me to meet you here."

"Clint Adams."

Heston straightened up and looked around.

"No, he's not here."

"Then where?"

"I can find him."

"And why would you want to?"

"He made a fool out of me and my partner, Lee."

"You fellas don't usually need help with that," Heston said.

"You're still a funny guy, Darby," Zack said. "You wanna hear this or not?"

"Yeah, okay," Heston said. "I came this far, I might as well listen."

"Okay," Zack said. "We was in a town called Evolution . . ."

***

"You're crazy," Heston said.

"You ain't afraid of Adams, are you, Darb?" Zack asked.

"Not me, idiot, but you should be," Heston said. "He'll kill you."

"Yeah, but not you," Zack said, "and not me if I'm with you."

"What about those others?" Heston asked. "And your partner?"

"You and me'll be partners, Darby," Zack said. "We're family. Them others can take care of the kid. Adams, he's ours."

"Ours," Heston said, staring at Zack.

"Yeah," Zack said.

Heston stared at his cousin a few moments more, then waved at the bartender and said to Zack, "Have a beer."

SEVENTEEN

Three days out and Clint was surprised when he woke up and found Roscoe nudging him with his foot.

"Coffee, and breakfast," the kid said.

He had switched watches with Roscoe each night, meaning the kid had to make breakfast this morning. It wasn't something he was used to doing, and Clint had assumed he'd have to wake up and do it.

When he approached the fire, he smelled coffee and beans. Roscoe handed him a cup, which he accepted gratefully.

Then he saw the mess of beans in the pan on the fire and knew what the kid had done.

"Smart guy," he said.

"What?"

"You made all of the beans for breakfast, Bookbinder," Clint said. "Means you want to stop at the next town for supplies."

"Jeez," Roscoe said, "is that the rest of the beans?"

"You know it is, Bookbinder."

With an innocent look on his face, Roscoe said, "Then we better eat 'em before they gets cold."

They sat their horses and looked down at the town of Ely, Kansas.

I've got a good mind to leave you here while I go in," Clint said.

"You wouldn't do that," Roscoe said hopefully.

"No," Clint said, "I wouldn't. Come on."

They started down the hill toward town, Roscoe all but kicking his mustang into a run.

"Take it easy," Clint said. "You've only been on the trail three days."

"Yeah, but I've learned a lot, right?"

"You've still got a lot to learn," Clint said.

"Like what?"

"Like not making all the beans for breakfast," Clint pointed out.

"Can we get some bacon this time?" Roscoe asked.

"We'll get bacon, Bookbinder," Clint agreed, "but just remember you better not cook it all next time it's your turn to make breakfast."

"I'll remember."

Ely was a very small town, pretty much just a mud hole in the road. It had a trading post, which also acted as a saloon, and not much else—except for a whore-house.

They pulled up in front of the trading post and dismounted. Across the street, on the second-floor balcony of the largest building in town, several women waved to them. One even bared her breasts.

"Whoa, look at that!" Roscoe said.

"Relax, lover boy," Clint said. "She'd probably give you a case of the crabs."

"The what?"

Clint shook his head.

"You do have a lot to learn. Come inside and have a drink."

Roscoe took one last, long look at the whore's breasts and then followed Clint inside.

There was a long counter made from two wooden doors. Behind it stood a tall, skinny man with a towel over his shoulder.

"Welcome, gents," he said. "Welcome to Jimmy's Trading Post. I'm Jimmy. What'll ya have?"

"You got any beer?" Clint asked.

"It's warm," Jimmy warned.

"I'll take it."

"I'll have whiskey," Roscoe said.

"He'll have a beer, too."

"If I'm gonna have somethin' warm, I'd rather have whiskey," Roscoe complained.

"I don't want you falling out of the saddle," Clint said.

"I can handle my liquor."

"We'll test that claim out another time, Bookbinder," Clint said. "Right now we'll have beer."

As Jimmy the bartender set the two beers in front of them, Roscoe said, "Some lady was showin' us her teats across the street."

"That'd be Lola," Jimmy said. "She's awful proud of those sweet things."

"Does she have crabs?" Roscoe asked.

"Hell, no," Jimmy said. "All those girls are clean as a whistle. We got us a sawbones comes in once a month to make sure." He leaned on the bar and looked at Roscoe. "You interested in one of them fillies for a little ride?"

"Let me guess," Clint said. "Is that Jimmy's Whorehouse across the street?"

Jimmy smiled.

EIGHTEEN

Clint actually believed Jimmy about the girls. A lot of whorehouses had taken to making sure their girls were clean so that men wouldn't get crabs or the clap and would come back.

He could see that Roscoe had the whorehouse across the street on his mind, the woman's—Lola's—naked breasts burned into his brain.

"You got a choice, boy," Clint said.

"What's that?"

"Food or sex," Clint said. "You can have a hot meal or a hot woman. Your choice."

"You get both right here, gents," Jimmy said. "Steaks?"

"A steak for me," Clint said. "Bookbinder?"

Roscoe walked to the window and looked out, then rubbed his stomach.

"Steak, I reckon."

Jimmy leaned forward and said to Clint in a low voice, "Reckon the boy's never had no pussy before, or he wouldn't make that choice."

"Just get the steaks," Clint said, "and they better be good."

"Best in town."

Considering they were in Ely, Clint figured that wasn't saying much.

"Get away from the window, Bookbinder," he called out. "You made your choice."

There were two tables across from the counter. Clint and Roscoe took one and Jimmy brought them each a steaming plate of steak and potatoes, and another beer each. The beer was still warm, but the steak was as good as Jimmy had promised. The potatoes, too. Soft and flavorful. The meat had just the right amount of blood running.

"You boys enjoy," Jimmy said. "And after, you can still go across the street if you've a mind to."

"After, we're going to need some supplies," Clint said. "If you give me some paper and pencil, I'll write out a list."

"You got a wagon, or a packhorse?"

"Just divvy it up into two canvas sacks," Clint said. "We'll each carry one."

"Whatever you say."

Jimmy left, and returned with the paper and pencil. After Clint wrote the list, Jimmy went to fill it and left them to finish eating.

"Why can't we go across the street?" Roscoe asked.

"I want to get back on the trail, continue your lessons"

"I could learn some lessons across the street," the kid said.

"Roscoe," Clint asked, "you ever been with a woman before?"

"Well, sure—"

"Don't lie to me, boy."

Roscoe looked down, pushed some spuds around his plate.

"No, I ain't."

Clint sat back. Maybe this would be another part of the boy's lessons.

"Finish your steak," Clint said, "and we'll see."

After they ate, Clint paid for the supplies and they carried the two sacks out to the horses and tied them to their saddle pommels. Then Clint turned and looked at the building across the street. The women were still on the second-floor balcony, and when they saw the two men watching them, not only did Lola bare her breasts, but they all did.

"Look at that!" Roscoe said in awe. "They're all doin' it!"

"I'm looking," Clint said. He had to admit it was an impressive sight.

"Okay," he said, "let's go on back inside, Book-binder."

"What for?"

"Well," Clint said, pointing across the street, "that's Jimmy's Whorehouse, so we have to go in and talk to Jimmy."

"About what?"

"About you being with one of his whores."

"Lola?"

"Sure, Lola," Clint said, "if that's what you want."

Clint turned to go back inside the building, and Roscoe nearly tripped trying to follow him.

NINETEEN

Lola took Roscoe into her room and said, "Don't be shy, sweetie. Take off your clothes."

Up close Lola was older than Roscoe had thought, probably over thirty. When he and Clint had gotten into the house, he'd spotted a nineteen-year-old blonde that appealed to him, but they had already paid for him to be with Lola.

She closed the door and turned to face him. He stood in the center of the room, still fully dressed.

"I think you need some encouragement," she said, unbuttoning her dress. "You want to see these up close?"

"Y-yes."

She pulled the dress open and her ripe breasts spilled out. Even the other girls in the house admitted that she had the best breasts there.

Roscoe licked his lips and his eyes widened.

"Do you want to touch them?" she asked.

"Yes."

"Kiss them?"

"Y-yes."

She closed her dress.

"Then you have to take off your clothes."

Roscoe didn't move or reply.

"Haven't you ever been naked before?"

"Well, yes."

"In front of a woman?"

He hesitated, then said, "Well, no."

She came close to him and said, "I'll help you."

She unbuttoned his shirt, leaning her head into him, tickling his nose with her dark hair. She opened his shirt and ran her hands over his chest.

"You're so hairless," she said. She reached down between his legs, rubbed him through his jeans. "I love young boys."

She undid his belt, unbuttoned his trousers, and then lowered his pants and underwear down around his ankles. His erect penis came into view and her eyes widened.

"I really like young boys," she said. "You're always so . . . ready." She took his penis in her hands. "And so hard . . . and long." From her knees she looked up at him. "This is very . . . impressive."

"Thank you."

His penis was very red and swollen. She opened her dress further, slid it down to her waist, and took his swollen penis between her breasts.

"Oh, God," he said, afraid that something was going to happen before it was supposed to.

She rolled his penis between her breasts, cooing to it, flicking her tongue out at it occasionally. She knew what she was doing, though, because she was careful not to let anything happen too soon.

"Get on the bed, sweetie," she said. "I'm gonna suck on that baby like it was a peppermint stick."

"Wha— Suck on it?"

"Just lay back, lover," she said, pushing him onto the bed. "You're gonna like it."

Roscoe wasn't sure what was going on, but he laid back on the bed and then watched while Lola took off all her clothes. When she was naked, he was surprised at how much dark hair there was between her legs, but he found himself excited by it.

She crawled onto the bed with him and rubbed her breasts up and down his legs, over his chest, the brown nipples as hard as pebbles. Finally, she settled between his legs, once again taking his swollen column of flesh between her breasts.

"You are so nice and big," she said, "and smooth. God, you're so young."

She swooped down, took him into her mouth for a quick suck, and then let him out.

She smacked her lips and said, "And you're so sweet!"

Before he could react, she took him in her mouth again, but this time she began to suck him avidly. He watched her and was shocked at how much of him she was able to take.

She continued to suck on him, and had a firm hold around the base of his cock. He closed his hands into fists and felt his toes curling. At one point his hands went to her head and held her there, and then he pulled them away when he realized what he was doing.

"You can touch, darling," she said, letting his penis slip wetly from her mouth. "You can touch me wherever you want."

She slid up onto him, sat on him so that his penis was trapped between them, and dangled her full breasts in his face.

"There," she said. "Enjoy."

He reached for them, held them in his hands, squeezed them, touched her nipples, but did not take them into his mouth until she leaned down even further and pushed them into his face.

"Come on," she said. "Taste 'em. Suck 'em, bite 'em. Let's have a good time!"

TWENTY

"What's the matter?" one of the girls in the parlor asked Clint. "Can't make a choice?"

"Well," Clint said, "after all, you're all so beautiful."

She laughed, a sound that Clint found oddly pleasing and soothing. He turned his head to take a better look at her. He had already sent four girls away, not because they weren't attractive, but because he had never paid for sex before, and he didn't intend to start today.

This one was in her late twenties and—unlike the others, who were attractive enough—she would have been lovely but for a scar that ran from her right eyebrow to the right corner of her mouth.

She smiled at him, though, and when she smiled the scar almost disappeared.

"What's your name?" he asked.

"Emily."

"How long have you been here?"

"A few months," she said. "I was passin' through,

got stranded, and they hired me. When I put some money away, I'll keep going."

"To where?"

"Just west," she said. "Maybe I'll end up in San Francisco."

"And do the same thing there that you're doing here?"

"Why not?" she asked. "It's honest work, isn't it?"

"Hey," he said, putting his hands up, "I'm not judging you, I'm just making conversation."

She calmed down and placed her hand on his knee.

"Would you like to continue it upstairs?"

"I don't think so, Emily," he said, "but thanks for the offer."

She sighed, retrieved her hand, and then looked around the parlor. The other men waiting there were either fat, old, dirty, or all three.

"Would it be so bad to pay for it, just this once?" she asked.

"I'm afraid I can't, Emily. Sorry."

"Well, all right."

She got up and walked across the room to where the least offensive of all the men was sitting. He looked like a big-bellied storekeeper who had taken the afternoon off.

Clint hoped Roscoe was learning a good lesson upstairs . . .

"Are you sure?" Lee asked Hector.

"Of course I'm sure," the Mexican said. "The tracks lead right into that town."

"Ely?" Lee said. "That's a town?"

"I know about it," Hector said. "It's got whiskey, beer, and whores."

"Then it's a town. Let's go."

"We can't go down there," Hector said.

"Why not?"

"Adams will see us."

"So what? He doesn't know who you are," Lee argued, "and neither does that kid. And maybe they won't remember me."

"What do you want to do down there anyway?" Hector asked.

"What do you think?" Lee asked with a grin. "I ain't been with a woman in a while."

"Well, I am not going," Hector said. "I will wait here for you."

"You're gonna make me go in alone?"

"I am."

Lee frowned.

Hector pressed on. "I will leave it to you to explain to Zack why you went down there."

The two men sat their horses and stared down at the few buildings.

"So what do you suggest?" Lee asked.

"We sit here and wait," Hector said.

"For what?"

"Well, for them to leave," Hector said, "or for Zack to show up."

"Zack," Lee said, "is back in Ellsworth with a cold beer and a hot whore."

Hector dismounted.

"I'm going to make a cold camp," he said. "You can do what you want."

"Jesus," Lee complained, "on top of everything else a cold camp?"

He hesitated, debating about what to do—cold camp or whiskey and a willing, paid-for woman—and in the end he dismounted.

TWENTY-ONE

"Again?" Lola asked.

"Yeah, again!" Roscoe said, hopping up onto his knees. "Lie back."

He pushed her down and she laughed, spreading her legs. He pressed the head of his penis against her wet portal and pushed. When he was inside, he began fucking her as hard as he could.

"I . . . really . . . do . . . love . . . young . . . men," she said into his ear.

Roscoe had heard other men talk about sex, but he'd never expected it to feel this good. He was simply amazed.

He slid his hands beneath Lola's ass and pulled her to him with each stroke. She alternately grunted and laughed, wrapping her legs around his waist.

"This . . . is . . . gonna . . . cost . . . extra, you know," she said.

"I don't care," he yelled.

"Come on, then," she exhorted him, "ride me, ride me harder . . . faster . . ."

He thought he was riding as hard and fast as he could, but in the next moment he discovered that he hadn't been.

"Whooee, that's it!" Lola cried.

"What's wrong?" Clint asked the madam.

"One of my girls says there's a lot of noise coming from Lola's room," the woman said. She was heavy, with lots of cleavage that looked like dough.

"So?"

"I'm just sayin' " she told him, "if your boy is doin' any harm—"

"Believe me," Clint said, "he's not doing any harm. He's probably just having a good time. It's his first."

"Oh," she said, rolling her eyes. "Why didn't you say so? Lola's probably got him shoutin' at the moon."

There was no moon, but he knew what she meant.

"No," Lola said, waving Roscoe away, "not again, lover. You've worn me out. Besides, I have to get back downstairs. I have other work to do, you know."

"Work?"

"That's what this is," she said, donning her dress. "That's why you pay me."

"But," Roscoe said, "I love you, Lola."

"Sweet boy," she said, touching his face. "You don't love me, you love what's between my legs."

"I love you for more than that."

She took his face in her hands and kissed him.

"Don't be a foolish boy," she said. "You'll have other women, other girls. Now get dressed. We have to go back downstairs."

Roscoe picked up his underwear and trousers and put them on, followed by his boots and then his guns.

"Come on, lovely boy," she said. "Follow me downstairs."

She held her hand out to him and he took it. She led him from the room.

"You what?" Clint asked as they left the building.

"I love Lola."

"No, you don't," Clint said. "You love what she has between her legs."

"That's what she said."

"Well, she's right," Clint said, "and so am I. Come on, we have some riding to do."

"Riding?" Roscoe asked. "Ain't we gonna stay in a hotel?"

"Look around you, Bookbinder," Clint said. "There is no hotel here."

"So we gotta sleep on the ground again?"

"That's right. And you're going to have the first watch."

"B-but . . . I'm exhausted."

"Yeah," Clint said, smiling, "I'm sure you are."

"Hey, hey," Lee said. "Look."

"What?" Hector asked.

"They're comin'."

Hector walked over to stand next to Lee and looked down toward Ely. He saw the two riders coming toward them.

"Crap!" Lee said. "They're comin' back the way they came."

"We have to break camp and move," Hector said. "And quickly!"

"Make camp," Lee complained, "break camp. I knew we shoulda went into town."

TWENTY-TWO

"What is it?" Roscoe asked.

Clint dismounted and held on to Eclipse's reins while he crouched down and touched the ground.

"Somebody made a cold camp here," he said, "and very recently."

"A cold camp?"

"A camp without a fire."

"Why would somebody do that?"

Clint waited until he was remounted before answering the question.

"Because they didn't want anyone to see their fire, smell their smoke."

"They were hidin'?"

"Apparently."

"From who?"

Clint shrugged. "Maybe us." He looked around.

"Whataya mean?"

"Somebody might be following us."

"What for?"

"What they usually follow me for," Clint said. "To take a shot at me."

"You mean, because of who you are?"

"That's right," Clint said. "That's what you have to look forward to if you get a rep with a gun, kid."

"Yeah, well," Roscoe said, "it must be worth it if you did it."

"I didn't have anybody telling me ahead of time what I had to look forward to," Clint said. "Nobody to warn me off."

"Well, I don't warn so easy."

"I get that," Clint said. "Come on, we'll have to stay aware of our surroundings."

"Keep an eye out, you mean?"

"Eyes, ears, nose," Clint said. "You've got to use all your senses out here, Bookbinder."

Roscoe started looking around, as if something would appear at any minute.

"And pay attention to the horses," Clint said. "They'll probably know something before you do."

"You always act like the horses are smarter than us," Roscoe said.

"Out here," Clint said, "they are."

"We are in trouble," Hector said.

"Why?" Lee asked.

"They know we were camped there."

"That don't matter," Lee said. "We're watchin' from a safe distance. They don't know who we are or where we are."

"But they know we are out here," Hector said. "Zack is not going to like that—and neither is his cousin."

"His cousin?"

Hector looked at Lee.

"You are his partner and you do not know his cousin?" Hector asked.

"We don't talk about families, Hector," Lee said. "Who the hell is his cousin?"

"Heston," Hector said, "Darby Heston."

"Heston? He never told me that! Jesus, it's bad enough he's got me mixed up with the Gunsmith, but Heston? Another gunny?"

"Heston is more than a *pistolero*," Hector said. "He is a killer."

"That's what it will take to kill the Gunsmith," Lee said. "I guess we're just along to take care of the kid."

Hector watched as Clint Adams and Roscoe Bookbinder began to ride off.

"That suits me," he said.

Zack and Heston watched as Randle and the others mounted up.

"Do we really need all of them?" Heston asked his cousin.

"Well," Zack said, "I wasn't all that sure you'd show up, Darb."

Both of them were mounted, waiting for the others. Heston looked at Zack.

"I wasn't sure I'd come either."

"So, if you didn't, I figured I needed some numbers n my side."

"If they get in the way—"

"If they get in the way, we'll get rid of them," Zack said.

"Just remember," Heston said, "Clint Adams is mine."

"Ours, Cousin," Zack said. "Clint Adams is ours. You're not the one he made a fool of."

"Okay," Heston said, "ours."

He ignored the others, turned his horse, and rode out of Ellsworth.

TWENTY-THREE

They camped that night, and over coffee and beans Clint told Roscoe, "We're being trailed."

"You know for a fact?"

"Yes."

"How?"

"I can feel them."

"You ain't seen 'em?"

"Not yet."

"But you can feel them?"

"Yes."

"Is that some kinda magic?"

Clint laughed.

"Maybe it is," he said. "It's a . . . it's just a sense you acquire after years on the trail."

"So what do we do?"

"I think we should ask them what they want."

"I thought you said when somebody was followin' you it was because they wanna take a shot at you?"

"Well, they haven't," Clint said, "and they've had their chances. So it's something else."

"And the only way to find out . . ."

". . . is to ask them."

"Now?"

"No," Clint said. "I don't want to wander around out there looking for their camp—especially if they're running another cold one. No, we'll make contact with them tomorrow."

Roscoe took out one of his guns and said, "And then we'll take care of 'em, right?"

"We're going to talk to them and see what they want," Clint said.

"And then we'll kill 'em?"

"Bookbinder, don't be in such a hurry to kill your first man," Clint said.

Roscoe holstered his gun, picked up his beans, and asked, "Who says it would be my first?"

"I told you before not to lie to me, Bookbinder," Clint said. "You're no killer. You may yet become one if I fail in what I'm trying to do, but you're not one now."

Roscoe hung his head and said nothing.

"Hey," Clint said, "not having killed a man yet is nothing to be ashamed of."

"You must think I'm just a stupid kid," Roscoe said glumly.

"I think you were probably on your way to becoming a stupid man," Clint said.

"And now?"

"And now, since you met me, that's not going to happen, is it?"

Sitting in their cold camp, a sullen Lee was cleaning his rifle.

"You know, I'm pretty good with this thing," he told Hector.

"I am sure you are."

"What about you?"

Hector looked at Lee. "What do you mean?"

"Can you shoot? With a rifle?"

"I am . . . competent."

Lee sat up straight and balanced his rifle on his knees.

"We could take him tomorrow," Lee said. "Before Zack, Heston, and the rest ever catch up to us."

"They will catch up tomorrow," Hector said. "Probably tomorrow afternoon. If we kill Adams, then we will be dead by tomorrow night."

"I'm not afraid of Heston," Lee said, "and I sure as hell ain't afraid of Zack. He's only my partner, he ain't my boss."

Hector didn't say anything.

"If you're afraid of Darby Heston, that's your problem," Lee muttered, sitting back.

"I am a very careful man, my friend," Hector said. "That is why I am sixty years old and still alive."

"Damn!" Lee said. "You're sixty? I thought you was about forty. You look good for your age."

"It is because I have lived such a careful life," Hector pointed out. "I do not bother sleeping snakes, *amigo*."

"You sayin' Heston's a sleepin' snake?"

"He is a killer," Hector said. "He is much worse than a snake."

"Yeah, well . . ."

"You do what you want tomorrow," Hector said. "I will do nothing to stop you."

"Yeah, well . . . ," Lee said again. "Maybe I'll just . . . wait."

Hector smiled to himself, unseen in the darkness, and said, "That sounds like a wise course of action."

TWENTY-FOUR

The next morning as they were saddling their horses, Roscoe asked, "How are we gonna do this?"

"We'll have to wait for a likely spot," Clint said.

"How do we find it?"

Clint mounted up and said, "I'll know it when I see it, kid. Let's go."

As Hector and Lee broke their cold camp, the Mexican asked. "Still going to wait?"

"Yeah," Lee said, "I thought about what you said about the sleeping snake."

In fact, Lee's whole attitude toward the Mexican had changed since he'd found out the man's age. Lee had always given credence to the advice of older men. His father was gone, he had no family, and Zack was his same age. He figured maybe Hector knew best in this case.

"Let's get moving, then," Hector said.

• • •

"One cold camp, and that's it," Heston said.

"The cold camp would be Lee and Hector," Zack said.

Heston pointed down at the town of Ely.

"That means Adams and the kid went to town," he said. "Probably for supplies."

"Maybe they're still there," Randle suggested.

Both Zack and Heston looked at him, but it was Zack who spoke.

"Look at that town," he said. "There's no hotel there."

"There's a whorehouse," Stride said. "I know, I been there."

Heston looked at Zack and nodded.

"Okay," Zack said. "Randle, you and Stride go down and check."

"What if they're still there?" he asked, alarmed.

"Even if they stayed, they ain't gonna still be there," Zack said.

"So why are we goin' down?" Stride asked.

"Find out if they were there, and if they said where they were goin'," Zack said. "That's it."

"But . . . Adams could still be there," Stride said.

Zack heard his cousin sigh.

"If he's still there," Zack said, "he doesn't know you. Don't do anythin', just catch up to us and let us know."

"Where will you be?" Stride asked.

"We'll be followin' the tracks from the cold camp," Zack said.

"Take the others with you if you're worried," Heston said, speaking for the first time. "You can all catch up later."

The men all exchanged glances, then shrugged. Better a whorehouse than the Gunsmith.

Heston and Zack watched as the four men rode down toward Ely. Zack looked at Darby Heston, whose eyes were boring holes into the backs of the men. He wouldn't have been surprised if his cousin had drawn his gun and mowed the men down, but he didn't.

"Don't worry, Zack," Heston said, as if reading his cousin's mind, "I'm not gonna waste my time killin' them."

"I didn't think—"

"Yes, you did," Heston said, cutting him off. "Besides, they'll probably never be able to find us again. You ready?"

"I'm ready."

They turned their horses and rode away from Ely.

TWENTY-FIVE

"Okay, stop," Clint said, holding his hand out.

"What?"

"This is the place," Clint said. "See this stand of trees? I'm going go wait here. You keep riding, and take my horse."

"But . . . where do I go?"

"Just go," Clint said. "It doesn't matter where, because I'll stop them here."

Clint dismounted and handed Eclipse's reins to Roscoe.

"Don't try to ride him or touch him, Bookbinder," he said. "He'll bite your hand off."

Roscoe accepted the reins and said, "How will I know when to come back?"

"You'll hear two shots."

"What if they kill you?"

"They won't," Clint said. "But if you hear more than two shots, you don't have to come back. Just drop Eclipse's reins so he comes for me, and keep going."

"You mean . . . abandon you?"

"If you want to."

"No," Roscoe said, "I'll come back, no matter how many shots I hear."

Clint smiled and said, "That's what I hoped you'd say."

Hector was looking down at the ground, following the trail. Lee was following behind, but his eyes were going everywhere. He saw the stand of trees they were approaching, but the thought of danger never occurred to him. After all, they were the pursuers.

"Hold it there, gents."

Both men froze. Hector looked up and saw Clint step from the trees.

"Both of you drop your guns."

Hector obeyed immediately. Lee hesitated. Clint fired two shots, one past each man—although they were really for Roscoe's benefit.

"Drop it, friend," Clint told Lee. "Don't make a mistake."

Lee removed his gun from his holster and dropped it to the ground.

"Now the rifles."

This time it was Hector who hesitated, but in the end he slid the rifle from his scabbard and dropped it. Lee was sliding his rifle out when they all heard the approach of horses. Clint knew it was Roscoe, but Lee thought it was Zack and the others and made a fatal mistake. He tried to bring the rifle around to bear on Clint, but Clint fired before he could complete the maneuver. Lee's body was knocked from the saddle, and struck the ground with a thud.

Roscoe came riding into view, leading Eclipse. Clint covered the Mexican.

"You want to make a mistake, too?"

"No, *señor*." The man raised his hands.

Roscoe came riding up and dismounted. "Are you okay?"

"I'm fine. You know that man?"

Roscoe walked over to the dead man and took a look.

"I think he was one of the men in the saloon that was raggin' me," he said.

"That's what I thought. Do you know *him*?"

Roscoe looked up at the Mexican. "I think I've seen him around town."

"Get down off your horse," Clint told Hector.

The Mexican complied.

"What's your name?"

"Hector Belasco Velez y Ramirez," the man said proudly.

"Goddamn Mexicans got the longest names I ever heard," Roscoe said.

"Hector," Clint said.

"*Sí, señor*."

"Why were you and your friend following us?"

Hector turned and looked at the fallen man.

"He was not my friend."

"Okay," Clint said, "partner, compadre, whatever. Why were you following us?"

"We were not," Hector said. "We were simply going in the same direction as you and . . . and your friend."

"You made a cold camp outside of Ely last night," Clint said.

"We did?"

"You were watching us, waiting."

"*Señor*—"

"If you're going to keep lying to me, I might as well put a bullet into you right now."

Hector smiled. Clint could see by the man's eyes that he was older than he looked.

"You would not do that."

"Why not?"

"I know your reputation," Hector said. "But I have not ever heard you called a cold-blooded killer. You kill men with guns in their hands."

"Pick up your gun then."

"I think not."

"The fact that you know my reputation means you know who I am," Clint said. "That means you were following us."

"Or it means I recognize you, *señor*," Hector said. "After all, you are a famous man."

"Maybe not that famous."

"Famous and modest."

"So you're not going to tell me who sent you to follow us?"

Hector didn't reply.

"Let me get it out of him," Roscoe said. "Let me kill him."

"What do you think, Hector?" Clint asked. "Think this kid would shoot you in cold blood?"

Hector looked over at Roscoe, who looked eager for the chance.

TWENTY-SIX

Clint decided to sit Hector down for a talk.

"You want me to make camp?" Roscoe asked.

"No camp," Clint said. "We're going to keep moving, but move that body into the trees so it's out of sight."

Roscoe swallowed. "Move the body?"

"Come on, boy," Clint said, "you're going to ruin your image in front of this man, and I need him to believe that you'd kill him if I told you to."

"Well . . . I would," Roscoe said.

"Okay, Bookbinder," Clint said, "then move that body, and those two horses."

"Okay."

As Roscoe tried to get the dead body up onto the man's horse, Clint walked over to where Hector was sitting, now with his hands tied behind him.

"Are you going to threaten to shoot me now that my hands are bound?" Hector asked.

"No, you were right, Hector," Clint said. "I don't

shoot unarmed men, but I can't say the same for my friend over there."

"He is young," Hector said. "He has killed no one."

"Oh, that much is true," Clint said. "I wouldn't try to fool you. He hasn't killed anybody—but he's eager to get started. He really wants that first notch on his gun. And it's up to me to decide if that's going to be you."

"You are trying to frighten me."

"I sure am," Clint said. "How else am I going to get you to talk?"

"I have nothing to say."

Clint noticed that as the man spoke he was looking back at the trail, the way he and the dead man had come.

"Obviously, you're expecting someone to come along," Clint said. "Were you trailing us just to keep us spotted for someone else?"

Hector stubbornly set his jaw.

"What's in this for you, Hector?" Clint asked. "There's no money. There's no price on either of our heads."

Roscoe came out from the clump of trees, hands on his guns.

"I get to kill him yet?" he asked.

"No," Clint said, "but we're getting closer."

"Aw, stand him up and give him his gun back," Roscoe said.

"You don't want me to leave his hands tied?" Clint asked.

"That ain't fair," Roscoe said. "I'll kill 'im fair and square. Give 'im his gun."

He drew both his guns, twirled them, and returned them to his holsters. The move surprised Clint. He hadn't seen the boy do that before.

"Roscoe, take a walk back a ways and check our back trail," Clint said. He could see the puzzled look on the boy's face, and headed him off before he could ask a question and betray his ignorance. "See if you can spot anyone, or any telltale dust clouds."

"Oh, okay," Roscoe said. "Then when I come back I can kill him?"

"Probably," Clint said. "Because I'm starting to think he's not going to talk."

Roscoe started walking and Clint turned back to Hector.

"You know what? Don't talk. I've got it figured anyway."

"You do?"

"That dead man was in the saloon, ragging on the kid. He had a partner with him. I stopped them. I figure I embarrassed them and now they're out for revenge, only they can't do it alone. So you and him were dogging our trail, waiting for his buddy to show up with some help."

Hector stared at Clint.

"The only thing I wanted from you," Clint said, "was for you to tell me who the help was, or how many there are, but that's okay. It doesn't matter now."

"And why is that?"

"Because however many there are, or whoever it is, my actions will be the same."

"And what will they be?"

Clint smiled. "You don't need to know that."

"Well, then," Hector said, "you might as well cut me loose and let me go, *Señor* Adams."

"Oh, I can't do that."

"Why not?"

"You'll just go and rejoin your friends, tell them that I killed that fella, and add your gun to theirs. I would be foolish to let you go. In fact, I'd be a damned fool to let you live."

For the first time the Mexican looked doubtful about the prospect of coming out of this alive.

TWENTY-SEVEN

Roscoe returned from checking their back trail, and Clint moved to meet him. He didn't want Hector to hear what they were saying.

"Anything?" Clint asked.

"I didn't see anybody," Roscoe said, "not even a puff of dust. Maybe you were wrong."

"Oh, they're coming, all right," Clint said.

"Did he talk?"

"No," Clint said, "it's not what he said, it's the look on his face."

"Are you always right?"

"No," Clint said, "but I am this time."

"So what do we do?" Roscoe asked. "Kill him?"

"We should," Clint said. "Do you want to do it?"

Roscoe shifted his feet uncomfortably. "You mean just outright? Like that?"

"We can leave him tied or, like you said, stand him up and give him his gun. You ready for that?"

Roscoe studied Clint for a few seconds, then said suddenly, "You want me to say no, don't you?"

"Why do I want you to say no?"

"Because that will mean I've learned somethin'."

"Right."

"And that my attitude has changed."

"Right again."

"So what do we do with him?"

"Well, I don't want him to let his friends know that we know they're coming," Clint said. "And I don't want him adding his gun to theirs."

"So if we don't kill him, what do we do?"

"We only have one other choice," Clint said. "We'll have to take him with us."

"The trail changes here," Heston said to Zack.

"How?"

"More horses," Heston said. "There are four horses now."

"So they caught up to Adams and the kid?" Zack asked.

Darby Heston looked at his cousin.

"More likely Adams let them catch up," Heston said. "Look, four horses, but only three move off."

"Where's the fourth?"

Heston pointed. "In those trees."

Zack stared.

"Well?" Heston asked.

"You want me to go in there?"

"It's just a stand of trees," Heston said. "You want me to hold your hand?"

Heston had dismounted to examine the ground. Now Zack dismounted and walked toward the trees.

He turned, looked at Heston over his shoulder, then drew his gun and walked into the trees.

Heston waited, watching the trail both behind and ahead. Moments later Zack reappeared, leading a horse with a man slung over the saddle.

"Who is it?" Heston asked.

"It's Lee," Zack said. "He's been shot."

Blood had dripped down the saddle, but had long since stopped yet had not dried.

"They're not that far ahead," Heston said.

"What about Lee?" Zack asked.

"Leave him," Heston said.

"We ain't gonna bury him?"

"No," Heston said. "We don't have time. Besides, there's a big cat around here somewhere. We might as well leave him to keep it busy. You want to take the time to bury him and let Adams get farther ahead?"

"No."

"Then take what we need from him and his horse and let's get going."

They rode with Clint in front, the bound Hector between them, and Roscoe taking up the rear, watching their back trail.

"If you go any faster, I will fall off my horse," Hector warned Clint.

"If you fall, I'll leave you on the ground," Clint said, "still bound."

"You wouldn't," the Mexican said. "My friends would catch up and release me."

"If they get to you before some critter does," Clint said. "I saw big cat tracks farther back."

Hector looked down at the ground. "Big cat?"

"Yeah," Roscoe lied, "I saw that, too." He didn't know if Clint had actually seen the tracks, but he decided to back him up.

"You want to take your chances with a cougar?" Clint asked Hector. "Or with us?"

TWENTY-EIGHT

"Aren't we takin' a chance makin' camp?" Roscoe asked Clint later that evening as the sun was going down.

"I don't think so," Clint said.

"Why not?"

"I think whoever's on our trail wants to kill me where people can witness it," Clint said. "What's the point of killing the Gunsmith if you don't get credit for it?"

"So he won't try to ambush you?"

"If that was the case, this one and his partner would have tried it," Clint said.

He pointed to Hector, who was still tied and sitting on the ground.

"*Señor* Adams is right," the Mexican said.

They both looked at him.

"Now you decide to talk?" Roscoe asked.

Hector gave a fatalistic shrug of the shoulders.

"It does not matter now," he said. "What will happen is fated to happen. Nothing I say can change that."

"So who's on our trail, Hector?" Clint asked.

Hector looked at Clint and shook his head. "Oh, that I won't tell you."

"Why not?" Roscoe asked. "I thought you said nothing you do can change what's gonna happen."

Hector remained silent.

"He knows that if he tells me who's coming, I'll recognize the name," Clint said. "If I recognize the name, I'll be ready."

"You would do well to listen to him, boy," Hector said. "He is a wise man."

"Bookbinder, see to the horses," Clint said. "I'll get the coffee and beans going."

"Are we gonna feed him?" Roscoe asked.

"Of course," Clint said. "I don't let a man go hungry."

He built a fire and got the meal going while Roscoe took care of the three horses. When Roscoe came walking over, Clint handed him a plate of beans.

"Cut him loose and let him eat."

"You givin' him a fork?"

"Let him eat with a wooden spoon," Clint said.

Roscoe took the beans, set them down, untied Hector's hands, and then handed him the tin plate with the wooden spoon. Hector put the plate down on the ground between his legs and rubbed his wrists.

"Can I have some coffee?" he asked. "*Por favor?*"

"Sure," Clint said. He poured a cup and held it out to Roscoe, who took it over to the Mexican.

"*Gracias.*"

Roscoe returned to the fire and accepted his own meal of beans and coffee from Clint. The three men ate.

Heston and Zack didn't bother with a cold camp. They made a fire and a hot meal of their own.

"If Adams wants to follow the scent of bacon, that's fine with me," Heston said.

"But we have to do this where people can see, Darby," Zack said.

"Don't worry," Heston said. "He won't come. He'll stay ahead of us, and wait for us to catch up."

"You think he knows we're comin' for him?"

"He knows somebody's comin' for him," Heston said. "How much he knows depends on what your friend Lee told him, or the Mexican."

"I don't know what Lee told him," Zack said. "He probably got himself killed before he could say anything. But Hector won't tell him a thing."

"Maybe you're right," Heston said, "but it don't really matter. We'll catch up to them sooner or later."

"Just the two of us?" Zack asked. "We can take him?"

"You take care of the kid, Zack," Heston said. "I told you to leave Adams to me."

Zack knew his cousin was fast with a gun. He'd seen him outdraw and kill two, even three, men at one time. And he was younger than Clint Adams. If anybody could put an end to the legend of the Gunsmith, it was Darby Heston.

•   •   •

Each night they camped, Clint would talk and Roscoe would listen. Each night Roscoe did more listening, and asked fewer questions.

That night Clint took the first watch. While Roscoe wrapped himself in his blanket, Clint took a blanket to Hector and made sure he was tightly bound.

"He asks a lot of questions," the Mexican said.

"He's listening more," Clint said, "and he's changing. If his attitude hadn't undergone a change already, he probably would have killed you, just for the experience of it."

"So your lessons saved my life," Hector said. "*Gracias.*"

"He still wants to try his hand, though," Clint said, looking over to where Roscoe lay. "He still wants to put those guns into play."

"He will get his chance," Hector said.

Clint looked back at Hector.

"How many are coming, Hector?"

"Enough so that you will need him," Hector said. "His baptism is coming."

Clint yanked on the man's bonds, making him flinch. He stood and dropped the blanket on top of him.

"I cannot say more," Hector said, "but I can give you some advice."

"I'll take it."

"Make sure you choose the time and place," the Mexican said.

"They do want it to be public, don't they?"

"Your humiliation of him—Zack—was public," Hector said. "His retribution must also be public."

"He hasn't got the nerve or the skill to pull this off," Clint said.

"He is bringing someone who has."

"I figured."

TWENTY-NINE

"We've got a choice," Clint said, standing in his stirrups. "That way is Abilene, and that way is a small town called Eager."

"I thought it was pronounced I-ger?" Roscoe said.

Clint looked at him, then at Hector, who shrugged.

"Just to avoid confusion," Clint said, "we'll go to Abilene."

"Good," Roscoe said.

"Why good?"

"Abilene's a big town, it's got newspapers," Roscoe said. "Whatever happens will be written up."

The boy's eyes were shining, and Clint knew he hadn't spent quite enough time with him—but how much more could he afford?

Clint had a quick decision to make. Go into town—Abilene, Eager, any town—or wait for his pursuers here? Which one would benefit the boy the most?

He decided to go into Abilene. Maybe the boy's final lesson would best be acted out in front of witnesses.

"Okay," he said. "Abilene."

"What are we gonna do with him?" Roscoe asked, indicating Hector.

"When we get to town, we'll turn him over to the sheriff," Clint said.

"For what?" Hector asked. "Following you? Is that a crime?"

"We'll think of something when we get there," Clint promised him.

When they rode into Abilene, Roscoe was wide-eyed. It was the largest, busiest town he had ever been in. He was surprised at the amount of traffic on the main street—horses, wagons, and pedestrians.

"I'll bet they have a really big whorehouse here," he said.

"More than one," Hector assured him.

"Shut up," Clint said to the Mexican.

"I've already seen three hotels," Roscoe said. "Which one are we gonna stay in?"

"Relax," Clint said. "First we'll stop at the sheriff's office and drop Hector off. Then, after we see to the horses, we'll check into a hotel."

Sheriff Aaron Carter placed Hector in a cell, then came back into his office, where Clint and Roscoe were waiting.

"So you have an idea who his partners are?" Carter asked. "Or when they'll get here?"

"No," Clint said.

"But you know what they want, right?"

"I can guess."

Carter frowned. He was in his fifties, had obviously been a lawman for many years in Abilene and in other towns. He'd been through this kind of thing before.

"So there's gonna be blood on my streets," he said.

"There's been blood on the streets of Abilene before, Sheriff," Clint said, "but there won't be this time if I can help it."

"I know how this works, Adams," the sheriff said. "They won't give you a choice."

"You never know, Sheriff," Clint said. "You never know."

Carter walked them to the door of his office.

"If you happen to spot them before they spot you, let me know, will ya?"

"Sure, Sheriff."

Outside the office, Roscoe said, "A hotel now?"

"I told you," Clint said, "the livery stable, then a hotel. Come on, we can walk them."

They grabbed the horses' reins and started walking. Clint had been to Abilene before and knew where the closest livery was.

"Why did you tell the sheriff there'd be no blood if you could help it?"

"Because there won't be."

"You won't fight them when they get here?"

"Not if I can avoid it."

"You mean . . . you'd run away?"

"I'd like to run away, Bookbinder," Clint said, "but I can't. If I did that, I'd be even more of a target for every two-bit gunny than I am now. No, I can't run, but I can try to avoid killing."

"But . . . why? You're fast. You can kill them easy."
The boy was truly puzzled.

"What if there's five of them?" Clint asked. "Or eight? Or ten? Should I stand in the street and face that many? That'd be stupid."

"But . . . what if there's only two, or three? You can kill that many, can't you?"

"Bookbinder, the day will come when one man with a gun will kill me."

"How?"

"He'll be faster. It could even turn out to be you."

"You think I could be faster than you?" Roscoe asked. "Really?"

Clint looked at the boy, then said, "You're not even listening," and walked on faster.

THIRTY

"Abilene," Darby Heston said.

"They're playin' right into our hands," Zack said. "You can kill Adams right in the street and it'll make newspapers around the country."

"Maybe."

"Whataya mean, maybe?"

Heston sat back in his saddle and regarded his cousin while rolling a cigarette.

"Why?"

"Why what?"

"Why is Adams goin' to Abilene?" Heston asked.

"It's a big town," Zack said. "Hotels, saloons, food, girls . . . why else would someone go there?"

"But by now he knows we're after him," Heston said. "Correction, he knows somebody's after him. He don't know it's me. He might know about you, but not me."

"Unless Hector told him."

Heston drew on his cigarette and squinted at Zack through the smoke.

"You told me the Mex wouldn't talk."

"Well, he wouldn't . . . normally."

"What's changed?"

Zack shrugged.

"He's in the hands of the Gunsmith," he said. "Maybe that'll impress him."

"It better not," Heston said, tossing the cigarette away.

"We goin' in?" Zack asked.

"We're goin' in."

They gigged their horses and rode to Abilene.

Clint and Roscoe got the horses into a livery and then they checked into a nearby hotel. It wasn't the biggest hotel in town, but to Roscoe it was the lap of luxury.

Clint knocked on Roscoe's door. He'd taken two rooms so the boy could have his own.

"Let's get something to eat," he said. "We've got time before they get here."

"This place is great!" Roscoe said as they walked down the hall.

"There's a restaurant across the street," Clint said. "Let's try that."

"I could use a steak this thick," Roscoe said, holding his thumb and forefinger a couple of inches apart.

"Then that's what you'll get."

"Really?"

"Why not?"

"This is great," Roscoe said. "I never had a steak that size."

They left the hotel, went across the street, and got a table in the moderately busy restaurant.

"Two steak dinners," Clint told the waiter. "All the trimmings."

"Comin' up. And to drink?"

"A pitcher of beer."

"Right."

As the waiter left, Roscoe leaned forward and said, "They bring a pitcher of beer to the table?"

"In some restaurants in large towns, yes," Clint said.

Roscoe sat back and said, "This is amazing."

"Settle down, Bookbinder," Clint said. "It's just a restaurant."

"Shouldn't we sit by the window so we can see the street?" Roscoe asked.

"No," Clint said, "I never sit by the window, because I don't want to be seen. Too easy to take a shot at me."

"Ah," Roscoe said.

"You won't have that problem, though—" Clint said, but Roscoe cut him off.

"I will when I get my reputation," he said.

"Bookbinder . . . ," Clint said, shaking his head. "Have you been listening at all the last few days?"

"Sure I have," Roscoe said. "I've been hearing you. It sounds to me like you wish you'd never picked up a gun, Clint. Like you wish you weren't the Gunsmith. Well, do you know what I wish? I wish I wasn't Roscoe Bookbinder. What the hell kind of name is that?"

"Roscoe—"

"So when I finally get my reputation, I'm gonna have a whole different name," he said. "I haven't picked it out yet, but you know how people make fun of me and call me the Two-Gun Kid? Even that name would be better."

The waiter came with two steaming steak plates, set them down, and then added the pitcher of beer and two glasses.

"Anything else?" he asked.

"No," Clint said, "no, I think we've got enough. Thanks."

Roscoe picked up his knife and fork and cut into his thick steak. Clint decided to suspend the lessons for a little while and just eat.

THIRTY-ONE

"We don't know where they are," Zack said, "or where they're stayin'."

"I'll find out," Heston said. "Don't worry."

"We can both find out."

They were at a rooming house on the edge of town. Heston had assumed they'd find at least one such place there. Most towns had them, he said to Zack. When Zack asked why they didn't just stay in a hotel, Heston said he didn't want to run into Clint Adams until they were ready.

"But he don't know you," Zack said.

"He knows you," Heston said. "At least, he saw you once."

"He might not remember."

"We're not takin' that chance."

So they found a rooming house being run by a widow named Mrs. Ivers, and they got two rooms. Now they were on the porch.

"I want you to stay here," Heston said.

"Where are you goin'?"

"Into town."

"I'm hungry, Darb."

"Mrs. Ivers will give you somethin' to eat," Heston told him.

"And you're gonna go to a restaurant, right? A café? And have somethin'? Maybe a steak?"

"I'm gonna see if I can locate Adams and the kid," Heston said.

"And maybe visit a whorehouse? Have a whore or two?" Zack asked.

"Yeah, maybe," Heston said. "What's the difference? I'm tellin' you to stay here. You understand?"

"Yeah," Zack said. "I understand."

Heston left Zack on the porch and walked toward the center of town.

"Look," Roscoe said over dessert, "I know you're tryin' to help me."

"I thought you asked me to help you," Clint reminded him.

"Well, yeah, I did, but I didn't think you were gonna try to change me," he said. "I just thought you'd help me learn to shoot, you know, better."

"Faster?"

"Yeah."

"More accurate, is more like it," Clint said.

"Yeah, yeah," Roscoe said, "I know, you been tellin' me, it's better to shoot straight than fast."

"So then you have been listening," Clint said, "at least part of the time."

"That's all we been doin', Clint, is talkin'," Roscoe said. "We ain't done much shootin'."

"That's because I wanted to work on your head first."

"Ain't nothin' wrong with my head."

"It wasn't screwed on tight enough, Roscoe."

"Huh?"

"You have to think more before you shoot."

"I'm worried about when there's no time to think," the kid said. "That's when I want to shoot fast and straight."

"Those times wouldn't come up if you weren't so intent on being a gunman, Bookbinder."

"There ain't nothin' else for me to be, Clint," Roscoe said. "I ain't gonna be no store clerk."

"There are other things you could be."

"No," Roscoe said, "there ain't."

Clint sat back, pushing away his empty dessert plate and beer mug.

"Okay," Clint said. "We've got another problem."

"Whoever's followin' us."

"Right."

"They're after you, right?"

"Looks like."

"But probably because you helped me back in Evolution when you did," Roscoe went on. "So I'm gonna stand with you."

"You may not have to," Clint said.

"Why not?"

"If there's one or two, I may not need you to," Clint said, "but if there's five or six . . ."

"I understand."

"So while we're waiting for them to get here," Clint said, "maybe we should do some more shooting and make sure you're ready for it."

"That's okay with me."

"You done here?"

Roscoe sat back and patted his belly. "I'm stuffed."

"Let's go find an empty lot somewhere," Clint said, getting up and digging for his money.

Darby Heston stopped short when he saw Clint Adams and the kid come out of a restaurant across the street. He recognized the Gunsmith because he'd seen him once before, a few years back. Also, Zack had described both him and the kid, Bookbinder.

Heston stepped back into a doorway. There was no way Clint Adams would know him on sight, but there was an off chance that Hector had described him. So he stayed back and watched Adams and Bookbinder walk down the street. When Heston realized he was standing in the doorway of a hotel, went inside and checked with the desk clerk. A dollar bought him the information that Clint Adams and Roscoe Bookbinder had registered, and each had his own room.

Since he now knew what hotel they were staying in, he walked across the street and entered the restaurant the two men had come out of. Both men had had their hands on their bellies. To Heston, that was the international sign that they had enjoyed their meal.

His cousin Zack had been right. Darby Heston wanted two things—a steak and, later, a whore.

THIRTY-TWO

Clint found an empty lot that was off Abilene's main street. It looked like a lot where a building had recently burned down, along with adjacent buildings, so there was no danger of errant lead going through somebody's window—unless it traveled blocks.

"Targets again?" Roscoe asked.

"Yes, but close up this time," Clint said. "I'm going to let you use your speed."

There was no fence, but there was a section of wall still standing. They walked to that wall. Clint looked around, found some boards, and propped them against the wall.

"The board is a man's torso," Clint said. "Hit it dead center."

"Not in the heart?" Roscoe said. He touched the board. "Right there?"

"No," Clint insisted, "dead center, Bookbinder. Send your bullet into the largest part of a man. You start to try to aim for parts—an arm, a leg, or the heart—you're going to get yourself—and me—into trouble."

"Okay."

"Just draw and fire when you're ready."

Roscoe spread his legs, drew his right pistol, and fired. He hit the board dead center.

"Other hand."

He holstered the right gun and prepared to draw the left.

"Reload first!" Clint snapped. "Don't ever return your gun to your holster with a dead chamber."

"Okay."

Roscoe drew the gun again, ejected the empty shell, replaced it with a fresh one, and then holstered the gun again.

"Okay, go," Clint said.

Once again Roscoe spread his legs and readied himself, then he drew with his left hand and fired. Off center.

"Again."

"Reload?"

"Later. Do it again."

Roscoe holstered the gun, drew, and fired. Not dead center, but better.

"Again," Clint said.

And again.

And again . . .

Darby Heston came out of the restaurant, rubbing his belly the way Clint Adams had been doing. The steak had been thick and tasty.

Heston decided to take a walk around town, maybe

locate Adams and the kid again. He wanted to watch Clint Adams for a while before he faced him. The reason Heston was still alive was that he always knew his enemy before he faced him. The other thing was he never let his stupid cousin get him killed. That was why he'd left Zack back at the rooming house.

He walked a few blocks and then heard shots. Following the sound, he found himself walking behind another man who seemed to be heading that way. Finally, they turned a corner and Heston saw Adams and the kid standing in an empty lot. He held back and watched as the other man crossed over to them. When the man turned in profile, just for a second, Darby Heston caught the glint of sun reflecting off his badge.

"You fellas mind if I ask what you're doin'?" the lawman asked Clint and Roscoe.

"Hello, Sheriff Carter," Clint said. "We're target shooting."

"Why?"

"Just to stay sharp."

"And are you expecting trouble?" the man asked. "Is that why you want to stay sharp?"

Clint and Roscoe exchanged a look.

"You never know when trouble's going to come, Sheriff," Clint said.

"And this has somethin' to do with the Mexican in my jail?"

"Oh, yes."

"You were supposed to come back and fill me in on that," Carter reminded him.

"We were going to come as soon as we finished here," Clint said.

"Let's do it now rather than later, Mr. Adams, shall we?" Carter asked. "Care to follow me?"

"Lead the way," Clint said.

THIRTY-THREE

"So you don't know who is comin' for you?" Sheriff Carter asked.

"Not by name, no," Clint said. "We know of at least one man who's coming. We had a set-to with him in a saloon in Evolution."

"Any reason to think he won't come after you alone?" Carter asked.

"One very big reason," Clint said. "He doesn't have the nerve."

"But you don't know the man."

"He didn't have the nerve in the saloon when he had another man with him to back his play," Clint said. "My guess is he's gone and found someone he can be confident with."

"Or more than one," Carter said.

"Yes."

"What about you, son?" Carter asked Roscoe. "You ready to back this man's play?"

"I'm the reason he's got somebody after him,

Sheriff," Roscoe explained. "He stepped in to help me in that saloon."

"So you'll back him?"

"I'll back him."

Carter looked at Clint.

"That's why you were target shooting in the lot?" he asked. "To keep him sharp?"

"Yes."

Carter looked at Roscoe again. "Son, have you ever killed anyone?"

Roscoe hesitated and looked at Clint, who nodded.

"No, I haven't."

"It's not an easy thing to do, you know."

"I know."

"Well," Carter said, "I'll just tell you that I've got three deputies and I'm not about to let you shoot up my streets, and my citizens."

"Fair enough," Clint said. "I'm not about to trade shots with anyone wearing a badge."

"Well, that's good to hear."

"That's about all I can promise you, though," Clint said. "If anyone else shoots at me, I'm going to shoot back."

Carter regarded him for a moment, then said. "Fair enough."

THIRTY-FOUR

As Clint Adams and Roscoe Bookbinder left the sheriff's office, Darby Heston once again backed into a doorway. He watched the two men cross the street and enter the Hickory Branch Saloon.

He waited.

Clint and Roscoe ordered a beer each and took them to a back table. The saloon was not large, and was not crowded. Finding a table was not hard.

"Back of the room," Roscoe said, "always."

"I don't have a choice in the matter, Bookbinder," Clint said. "Neither will you, if—"

"Yeah, yeah, I know," Roscoe said, "if I decide to live by the gun."

Clint studied the young man. He wondered what the act of killing a man would do to Roscoe Bookbinder. Would he feel sick, regretful, and put his guns down? Or would he like it, and have a taste for blood after that?

"So what do we do?" Roscoe asked. "Just wait?"

"That's right, we just wait."

"How about a whorehouse?" the kid asked. "Why don't we go to a whorehouse?"

"Why don't you?"

"You mean it?" Roscoe asked

"Yeah," Clint said. "I'm not interested, but you go ahead. You need money?"

"No, I got money," Roscoe said. "It ain't gonna be too much, is it?"

"More than before," Clint said, "but not too much."

"Okay." He stood up. "You sure you don't wanna come?"

"Have a good time," Clint said, "and keep your eyes open on the street."

"I will," Roscoe said. "I'll see you back at the hotel."

Clint had second thoughts about letting Roscoe walk the streets alone, but he felt sure that their pursuers were after him, not Roscoe Bookbinder.

Clint decided to walk the street himself. Maybe without Roscoe he could get this all taken care of. Maybe if he showed himself, they'd try for him while the kid was in the arms of a warm, willing prostitute.

He paid his bill and went out on the street.

Roscoe found a whorehouse with no problem. All he had to do was ask the bartender on the way out.

"Ask for Mandy, and tell 'er Joe sent ya, from the Branch. She'll know."

"Thanks."

He followed the bartender's directions—two blocks south, then west for two blocks—and found the house, a two-story wood-frame with three steps leading up to the front door. He mounted the steps and knocked. When the door opened, he was looking at a huge, bald black man.

"What you wan'?" the man asked.

"Uh, Joe sent me, from the Branch. Told me to ask for Mandy."

"Huh," the black man grunted, but he opened the door. "Come on in."

Roscoe entered and the man closed the door behind him, then looked at him.

"You old enough to be here?" he asked.

"I'm twenty-two."

"Dat's old enough, I guesses," the black man said. "Go ahead, inta the parlor."

Roscoe found the parlor very familiar. It was like the one in Evolution, only bigger, with more girls. He made his choice very quickly. A young girl, about his own age, slender and pretty. She didn't have the same charms Lola had, didn't have the big breasts, but he was attracted to her from the beginning.

"Have you made your choice?" an older woman asked him. She had big breasts like Lola, only they were starting to sag under their own weight. She had to be at least fifty.

"Are you Mandy?"

"That's me."

"Joe sent me over."

"Joe's a good friend," she said.

Roscoe was staring at the young girl. Mandy followed his gaze.

"Ah, I see you've spotted Betsy."

"Betsy?"

"She's new here," Mandy said, "but she's very good. She's about your age, too."

"Um, okay, yeah."

"What's your name?"

"Roscoe."

Mandy waved at Betsy, who came sashaying over. Close up, she was even prettier, and Roscoe found himself holding his breath.

"Betsy, this is Roscoe."

"Hello, Roscoe," Betsy said, extending her hand. He hesitated before shaking it.

"This is Roscoe's first time here," Mandy said.

"But not my first time," Roscoe hurriedly added.

"No," Mandy said, "of course not. He's very interested in going upstairs with you."

"Is that right, Roscoe?" Betsy asked.

"Yes."

"I'm very flattered," she said, sliding her arm through his. "Come on, then. I have a very nice room, with a big bed."

She led him to the stairway just outside the parlor and up to the second floor.

"Will you do me a favor before we go to my room?" she asked.

"What's that?"

"I just put clean sheets on the bed," she said, "and you obviously just came in off the trail."

"Yeah."

"Would you mind taking a bath first?"

Roscoe hesitated.

Then she added, "With me?"

THIRTY-FIVE

Roscoe watched from the tub as Betsy dropped her robe to the ground and joined him, naked. Her breasts were small, pert, tipped with pink nipples. The hair between her legs was paler brown than the hair on her head, and sparse. Her skin was smooth and very white. As she sat in the tub, her legs rubbed against him, and they felt impossibly smooth.

"Come here," she said. "Scootch down."

He slid toward her. She grabbed a washcloth and a bar of soap and began to wash his chest and shoulders and neck. Eventually, she moved down to his belly, and then concentrated on his crotch.

"Wow," she said, as his erection broke the surface of the water and kept going. "That's a long one."

"Is that okay?" he asked.

She took him in her hands, stroked him up and down, and said, "It's fine, Roscoe." She squinted at him. "Is this really not your first time?"

"It really isn't."

She studied him, her hands bringing his penis to

even greater heights than Lola had been able to achieve.

"Second time?"

"Yeah," he said, catching his breath, "second."

She moved her hands, with the cloth, down beneath the water and began to wash his testicles, then moved down his thighs and his legs, finally ending at his feet. All the time his erection bobbed above the water.

"There," she said, "now all we have to do is wash your hair, and then you and I can go to bed."

"M-my hair?"

"Could use a cut, too," she said, "but I don't do that here. Come on, lean down."

Clint returned to the Hickory Branch and had another beer at the bar. He now knew there was somebody outside watching him. Whoever it was had been following him and Roscoe for a while, and had followed him when he left the bar earlier. And whoever it was he was very good, because although Clint could feel him, he hadn't spotted him yet. And he probably wouldn't. It was more likely the man would approach him at some point, so he'd decided to stand at the bar and make it easy.

Darby Heston stood across the street from the Hickory Branch Saloon. He had seen the kid, Bookbinder, leave and had let him go. It wasn't him he was interested in, just the Gunsmith. He'd followed him earlier, outside and then back here.

He could see through the window that Adams was

standing at the bar, and suddenly he knew that the Gunsmith was waiting for him. He probably knew he was being followed, but Heston knew he was good at it: Adams hadn't seen him, so he was waiting for him.

So now the question was, should he go ahead into the Hickory Branch and face the man? Not with his gun, but just for a talk?

Why not? It would be totally in keeping with his know-your-enemy philosophy. And it would show Adams that he wasn't afraid of his reputation. After all, Darby had a reputation of his own.

He quit the doorway he was standing in, stepped into the street, and walked across to the Hickory Branch Saloon.

As Heston entered the saloon, Clint called the bartender over and said, "A beer for my friend."

THIRTY-SIX

"Thanks," Heston said, picking up the beer.

"Following somebody, waiting in doorways," Clint said, "it can be thirsty work."

"It sure can."

"You obviously know who I am," Clint said. "Do I get to know who you are?"

"Heston, Darby Heston."

"Heston," Clint said, frowning, "I know that name."

Heston didn't speak, but he felt kind of proud that the Gunsmith had heard of him.

"I don't know where from, but I've heard it," Clint said.

"I have a . . . reputation," Heston said, seething now because he thought Clint was disrespecting him.

"Really?" Clint asked. "As what?"

"With a gun, like you."

"Lots of men think they have a rep with a gun, Heston," Clint said.

"Well, I do."

"So now you're after me?"

"That's right."

"Why?"

"One of those idiots you faced down in Evolution was my cousin."

"And where is he?"

"Around."

"Just the two of you?"

"There are some more idiots on the way," Heston said, "but I thought I could handle this by myself."

"Really?" Clint said. "Is that a fact?"

"Yeah, it's a fact."

"Are you going to try the kid first?" Clint asked. "You know, he just might kill you himself and save me the trouble."

"That's a laugh," Heston said. "No, I ain't interested in the kid, Adams. Just you."

"Do you want to do this now?"

"No," Heston said. "It can wait."

"Until when?"

"Until I'm ready," Heston said. He'd regained his composure, having realized that Clint was baiting him. He finished the beer and put the mug down. "Thanks for the drink."

"Anytime."

Betsy took her time drying Roscoe with a big fluffy towel. She spent a lot of time on his balls and penis, almost driving the poor kid into a frenzy.

"There," she said finally, "now we're both dry enough for the bed."

"Then let's get in it!" he said impatiently.

He grabbed her and hauled her to the bed. She was very light, and she squealed as he picked her up.

On the bed, he tried to stuff his eager penis into her, but she closed her thighs and said, "Wait, wait. Take your time, darling."

"I can't," he said. "You been teasin' me since I got here and I can't wait no more."

"Well," she said, opening her thighs with a smile, "in that case . . ."

He drove his long, rigid cock into her, and she squealed again . . .

The bartender came over and asked Clint, "Another one?"

"Sure."

The bartender placed a full mug in front of him and asked, "Problems?"

"Aren't there always?"

"I couldn't help overhearing," the man said. "Ya want my advice?"

Clint looked at the man, then picked up the beer and said, "Okay, sure. Let's have it."

"Either he's gonna kill you, or you're gonna have ta kill him."

"That's advice?"

"That's an observation," the man said. "Here comes the advice." He leaned forward and lowered his voice. "Kill him first."

"First?"

"Yup," the bartender said. "Any way ya can. Just get

to him first. I mean, he looks like a pretty mean hombre, to me."

"Yeah," Clint said, "you're probably right. He is probably a mean hombre." He raised the mug and said, "Thanks."

THIRTY-SEVEN

When Heston got back to the rooming house, his cousin Zack practically attacked him.

"Where the hell have you been?" he demanded. "I been goin' crazy here."

"I've been around."

"Around? Doin' what?"

"Well," Heston said, "I followed Adams and the kid for a while, and then I had a talk with Clint Adams."

"A talk? Are you crazy? He . . . he talked to you? Without goin' for his gun?"

"Of course he talked," Heston said. "We're both pros. We had a beer together and got to know each other a little."

"Got to know each other?" Zack looked like his eyes were going to pop out of his head.

"You got to know a man before you kill him, Zack," Heston said. "You don't just walk up to a man and shoot him."

"Hell ya don't," Zack said. "You do when it's the

Gunsmith. Jeez, why give him a chance to kill you first, Darb?"

"That's not gonna happen, Zack," Heston said. "Now, stop yelling at me before I put a bullet in you!"

"Okay," Zack said, regaining his breath and his composure, "okay, ya don't have ta put a bullet in me, Darb."

"Did the old lady feed you?"

"Yeah," Zack said. "I had some beef stew. It was real good, too."

"That's good. She gonna make us breakfast, too?"

"Yeah," Zack said. "Eggs, potatoes, biscuits . . . everythin'."

"Okay, good," Heston said. "Tomorrow's gonna be the day I kill Clint Adams, and I want to do it on a full stomach."

"Tomorrow? Really?"

"Yeah, really," Heston said. "Tomorrow we'll take care of both of them, and make a name for ourselves."

"Darb . . . you sure you don't wanna wait for the others?"

"The others are idiots, Zack," Heston said, and added to himself, *like you.* "We don't need them. We can take care of this ourselves. I'm going to my room now. Don't bother me until breakfast tomorrow. Got it?"

"I got it."

"And don't you leave here," Heston added. "I don't want you going into town and getting yourself shot. You got that?"

"I got it, Darb," Zack said, "I got it."

• • •

"You want me to do what?" Roscoe asked Betsy.

"Put it in me from behind." She got on her hands and knees and looked at him over her shoulder. "Like this."

"But . . . ain't that dirty?"

"No, it ain't dirty," she said. "Besides, I ain't askin' you to put it in my ass. I want you to put it into my pussy from behind."

"I can do that?"

"Just get over here and slide that big stick up between my thighs. I'll do the rest."

"Like this?"

He slid his penis up between her thighs. She grabbed it, held on to it, and backed up onto it, taking it inside her.

"Ah, that's it!" she gasped.

"Jeez," he said as he was engulfed by her heat.

"Come on!" she said, slamming her butt back into him. She kept moving back and forth, back and forth, until he found her rhythm and began to move with her. After that, the sound of flesh slapping flesh filled the room, with the grunting of both of them mixed in.

"Oh jeez," Roscoe yelled, taking hold of her hips and holding tight.

"This as good as your first time, baby?" she asked.

"Oh, this is better," he said, "much better!"

Betsy laughed and quickened their pace. Roscoe's breathing started to get ragged.

"Come on, my stud," she called. "You're a young stallion. Keep up with me."

"I'm . . . keepin' . . . up with . . . you . . . ," he said, gritting his teeth.

She was getting so wet that her juices were running down her thighs and soaking the sheets. Abruptly, she pulled free of him, turned onto her back, and opened her thighs wide.

"Come on, baby," she said. "This ride ain't over."

He got between her legs, pressed the head of his penis to her soaking portal, and drove it in.

"Oh, yeah!" she shouted.

"Yes!" he yelled. "Yeahhhhh . . ."

THIRTY-EIGHT

Clint was sitting in a wooden chair in front of the hotel when Roscoe showed up several hours later. The kid looked clean, and worn out.

"How was it, Bookbinder?"

"It was . . . amazing," he said. "Is it always like that?"

"No," Clint said. "Even when it's bad it's good, but it isn't always amazing."

Roscoe pulled over another chair and sat down next to Clint.

"What did you do?"

"Drank some beer, got some advice from a bartender, talked to the man who's been tracking us."

"What? Wait, you talked to him?"

"Yep."

"So you know his name?"

"Yes, it's Darby Heston."

"Wait," Roscoe said again. "I know that name, don't I?"

"I think you do," Clint said. "He's from your neck of the woods and he has a rep with a gun."

"Heston, that's right!" The kid's eyes glittered. "I could take him, Clint."

"No way, Bookbinder."

"What?"

"You're not ready to face a man with a rep."

"B-but you been teachin' me—"

"You've hardly learned anything, kid," Clint said. "If I let you face Heston now, you're a dead young man."

Roscoe came up out of his chair.

"Settle down, kid."

Roscoe folded both hands into fists and faced Clint, but his rage was impotent.

"If I can take Darby Heston, my rep will be made, Clint."

"Kid, I can't let you—"

"This ain't fair!" Roscoe shouted, and stormed off into the hotel.

Maybe it wasn't fair, but Clint wasn't about to let the kid get killed facing Heston alone, or any other gunny with a rep.

He decided to stay outside for a while, then check with the kid later to see if he settled down.

THIRTY-NINE

Roscoe wouldn't answer his door when Clint knocked, so he went to bed without talking to the kid. In the morning he knocked again, and there still was no answer. He had started down the hall, intending to go downstairs for breakfast, when a thought struck him. He retraced his steps, knocked on the door, then pounded on it.

"Come on, kid!" he called, but there still was no answer. He thought about kicking the door in, but didn't think he had to. The kid just wasn't there.

He went down to the lobby and asked the desk clerk when Roscoe had left the hotel.

"About half an hour ago, sir."

"Damn it!"

He went out the front door. He knew what the kid was doing; he was walking the streets looking for Darby Heston. Maybe Roscoe was even checking hotels and rooming houses. If he managed to find Heston, Roscoe was a dead man for sure.

Clint picked a direction and started walking.

• • •

Roscoe Bookbinder was still fuming from the night before as he walked the streets of Abilene, looking for Darby Heston. He was going to find the man and call him out, even if he had to check every hotel and every rooming house in town.

"Nope," a desk clerk told him, "nobody with that name stayin' here."

"I'm sorry," an older woman told him, "I ain't rented a room to anybody by that name. In fact, all my rooms are empty. Are you interested?"

He turned and left as she called out that she would give him a discount.

He'd been at it for better than half an hour, but Abilene was a big place. And he was prepared to try all day.

At breakfast in the rooming house, Zack said, "So today we take care of the Gunsmith?"

"I got a better idea," Heston said.

"What?"

"Let's take care of the kid first," Heston said.

"Why?"

"Because it'll give us an edge over Adams," Heston said.

"He'll be really mad."

"Yep," Heston said, "too mad to see straight."

Zack grinned. "I getcha. When?"

"Finish breakfast," Heston said. The table was covered with eggs, bacon, biscuits, and flapjacks. Nobody else was there because at the moment they were the only guests. "Our landlady was nice enough to put this spread out for us. Let's finish it, and then go find the kid. You remember what he looks like, right?"

"Oh, yeah," Zack said. "The kid's a joke. Wears two guns with pearl handles."

"Can he use them?"

"Naw," Zack said. "He's an amateur."

"Good," Heston said, "then you get to kill him."

"Good," Zack said. "He's the reason Adams made fools out of me and Lee in the first place."

"Eat some more of them flapjacks," Heston said. "We don't want them to go to waste, do we?"

Zack speared several of them with his fork and said, "No, we don't."

Clint walked right by Sheriff Carter before he realized who it was. He stopped and turned to find the man looking at him.

"You're in a hurry, Mr. Adams," Carter said.

"Have you seen Roscoe Bookbinder?"

"Bookbinder? The kid that was with you?"

"Yes."

"Not today. Why?"

"I talked with Darby Heston last night."

"Heston?" Checker asked. "I know who he is. What's he doin' in town?"

"Looking for me apparently."

"He's the one?"

"Yes."

"What's this got to do with your missin' young friend?" the sheriff asked.

"I'm afraid Roscoe is out looking for him."

"That's just great," Carter said. "Okay, keep lookin'. I'll get my deputies and we'll scour the town for him."

"Okay, thanks."

"Look," Carter said as Clint started to walk away, "when I find him, I'm gonna toss his ass in a cell for his own good."

"With my blessing!" Clint called back over his shoulder.

FORTY

Walking the streets of Abilene . . .

Roscoe Bookbinder, looking for Darby Heston . . .

Heston and Zack, looking for Roscoe . . .

Clint Adams, looking for Roscoe . . .

The sheriff and his deputies, looking for Roscoe Bookbinder, or any suspicious-looking gunmen . . .

Clint decided to change his tactics. He stopped looking for Roscoe and started looking for Darby Heston, probably in the company of another man—a man Clint had seen in the saloon in Evolution.

Two men with guns, searching either for him or for Roscoe. If he was Darby Heston, he'd kill Roscoe first, hoping to get into Clint's head and thereby gain an edge over him when it came time to face him.

And then he saw them—Heston and a second man—across the street. He recognized the man from Evolution.

Clint looked around him. No sign of anyone with a badge, and no sign of Roscoe Bookbinder.

If he faced Heston and the other man now, and killed them, he would probably be saving Roscoe's life, but would he be teaching the boy anything?

Perhaps, he thought, it was more important to keep him alive. He could worry about teaching him a lesson later.

He stepped into the street and started across . . .

"Adams!" Heston said.

"What?" Zack asked. "Where?"

"Comin' across the street," Heston said. "Right for us."

"Then you'll kill him now? And we can take care of the kid later?"

"I don't know," Heston said, turning to face Clint Adams. "I guess that'll be up to him."

"Darb—"

"Shut up, Zack," Heston said, waving at his cousin. "Shut up and let me do the talkin'. Just stand there and listen. Got me?"

"Yeah, Darb," Zack said, "yeah, I got you."

As Clint reached them, the two men turned to face him, but it was clear that the second man was simply going to stand by and watch. He was standing just a few steps back—but not behind Darby Heston

"Heston," Clint said.

"Adams."

"You look familiar," Clint said to the other man.

"My cousin Zack."

Zack remained silent.

"Ah," Clint said, "it's a family thing."

"So?"

"You out looking for Bookbinder?" Clint asked.

"Who?"

"He knows," Clint said, indicating Zack.

"Oh, your young friend?" Heston said. "Why? Is he out lookin' for us?"

"He is," Clint said, "but I'm not going to let him face you."

"And how are you gonna do that?" Heston asked. "By facing me yourself?"

"If that's what it takes."

"That's what it'll take," Heston said. "And I'll kill him anyway, after I kill you."

"So I guess I don't have much choice," Clint said.

"Not much, I guess."

"In the street?"

"Why not?" Heston asked. "That's where this stuff usually takes place."

"Darb—" Zack started, but Heston cut him off with a wave.

"Don't get in the way, Zack."

That actually suited Zack. He'd been saying all along he wanted to be part of the action when Heston took on the Gunsmith, but now, in the face of it actually happening, he was happy to step back.

Clint and Heston stepped into the street. The people of Abilene had seen many face-offs of this kind, and they instinctively knew something was happening. They cleared the street and lined up along the boardwalk on either side. Some of them closed their doors to avoid flying lead, but still went to their windows to stare.

They were on Main Street, so the crowd along the sides grew pretty large in a short time. But there still was no sign of any badges.

The street was pitted with holes and wheel ruts, but dry, since there had been no rain for a while. A bit of wind made some of the dust swirl around their feet.

Clint and Heston took positions in the center of the street. Clint actually hoped they'd be able to get this done before either Roscoe or the sheriff came along. Once a killing looked inevitable, he liked to get it over with.

"Anytime, Adams," Heston said. "You're older than me, so you go first."

"You're a fool, Darby," Clint said. "Don't ever give a man the first move—especially a better man."

"I'll show you who the better man is," Heston said.

His hand streaked for his gun. Clint was impressed by the man's speed, even as he outdrew him and shot him dead center in the chest. Heston stepped back, coughed, frowned, dropped his gun, and fell to the ground.

"No!"

Clint turned and saw Roscoe running toward him. "He was mine!"

Roscoe stopped and looked down at Darby Heston, who was dead.

"You want to kill somebody, Bookbinder?" Clint asked, replacing his spent shell with a live one. "Kill him." He pointed to Zack. "He's Heston's cousin."

Roscoe turned and looked over at Zack.

"Is your name Heston?" Roscoe asked.

"N-no," Zack said. "I don't—didn't—have the same last name as him. My name's Foley."

"Foley," Roscoe said, as if the name tasted bad in his mouth.

"It doesn't matter," Clint said. "He's still Heston's cousin. Go ahead. Face him."

Roscoe took a few steps toward Zack. The people near him on the boardwalk scattered, leaving Zack standing alone.

"Step in the street," Roscoe said. "Come on."

Zack noticed that Roscoe's clothes were not as silly-looking as they had been, and he saw that the pearl handles were gone.

"Uh, n-no, no," Zack said, "I ain't got any beef with you, kid."

"Well, I got a beef with you!"

"No, no—" Zack said, holding his hands out.

"Hold on there!"

They all turned and saw Sheriff Carter running toward them with his deputies. They all had their guns out. Clint holstered his.

"That Heston?" Carter asked Clint.

"That's him."

"Dick," Carter said to one of his deputies. The man walked over and checked Heston's body.

"He's dead, Sheriff."

"Then it's all over," the sheriff said.

"What about him?" Roscoe demanded, pointing at Zack.

The sheriff turned and looked at the other man.

"I got no beef with these fellas, Sheriff," Zack said.

"Then I suggest you get out of Abilene, son," Carter said. "Now!"

"Yessir!"

Zack turned and ran.

Carter looked at Roscoe.

"You ain't gonna get to kill anybody today, boy," he said.

Roscoe turned, threw a murderous look at Clint, then stalked off.

"Don't think that young fella is very happy with you, Adams."

"I guess not."

"Can't say as I am either," the lawman added. "Time for you to leave town, too."

"I guess so," Clint said.

"Take the boy with you, if he'll go."

Clint nodded and said, "If he'll go."

FORTY-ONE

Clint found Roscoe in his room. When he knocked, the boy didn't answer, but the door was unlocked, so Clint walked in.

"You didn't have no right to do that!" Roscoe shouted as Clint entered.

"I had every right to keep you alive."

"You ain't my pa," Roscoe said. "You ain't nothin' to me."

"That's fine," Clint said. "I'm leaving anyway. The sheriff asked me to take you with me, but—"

"I ain't done nothin'," Roscoe said. "I don't gotta leave."

"That's fine, too," Clint said. "I just . . . wanted to say good-bye. I just hope you've learned something, Bookbinder."

"Yeah," Roscoe said, "I learned not to trust you anymore."

Clint stared at Roscoe, who turned away and stared out the window. Clint left.

In the hall he figured he was going to have to be

satisfied with saving the boy's life, but he was afraid
that the rest of the time he'd spent with him had been
wasted, for both of them.

Zack was riding out of Abilene when he ran into Eric
Stride, Ken Randle, and the other two.

"What the hell—" Stride said. "We been lookin'
for you for days."

"Where's your cousin?" Randle asked.

"Darby's dead," Zack said. "The Gunsmith killed
him."

"Outdrew him?"

"Clean," Zack said. "Fastest thing I ever saw."

"Jesus," Stride said. "Look, Zack, we ain't about
to face the Gunsmith—"

"I don't want you to," Zack said, "but I do wanna
kill the kid that's with him."

"How do we do that?" Randle asked.

"Easy," Zack said. "We ride into Abilene and do it,
and then we ride out."

"That easy?" Stride asked.

"That easy."

"And Adams?"

"He'll be gone," Zack said. "Sheriff ran both him
and me outta town."

"Are we gonna have to deal with the law?" Stride
asked.

"Not if we do it like I said," Zack told him. "In and
out."

"And what do we get out of it?" Randle asked.

"A reason for ridin' all this way," Zack said. "Oth-
erwise you wasted a helluva lot of time."

"He's right," Stride said. "Killin' that kid will at least make it worth it."

He looked at the others, who shrugged their approval.

"Why not?" one of them said.

"There's five of us," Zack said, turning his horse to face town again. "I ain't gonna be run off again."

Zack, Stride, Randle, and the others were north of town. When Clint rode out, he rode south.

Without knowing that Roscoe Bookbinder was going to face five men all by himself.

FORTY-TWO

Hard Ace Saloon, Ellsworth, Kansas

When Clint entered the Hard Ace Saloon, he had already been to both Evolution and Abilene.

He went to Abilene after he heard about the lone gunman who was shot down by five others in the street. He got the story from Sheriff Carter . . .

"They rode in soon after you left," Carter said. "There wasn't anything I could do. Me and my deputies were at the undertaker's, delivering Heston's body. Those five just rode in, found your kid, and shot it out with him."

"Shot it out?"

The sheriff nodded.

"Witnesses said he tried to give as good as he got, he was just outnumbered." The lawman shook his head. "They shot him to pieces."

"And you didn't bother to try to track them down with a posse?"

Carter shrugged.

"It was a shooting, Adams," he said. "Your boy was looking for a shooting, wasn't he?"

"Yeah," Clint said, "but he wasn't looking for a massacre."

After leaving Abilene, Clint rode back to Evolution to tell Roscoe's uncle, Sheriff Greenwood, that his nephew was dead.

"I heard," Greenwood said from behind his desk. "It was bound to happen."

"You got any interest in finding the men who did it?" Clint asked.

"It didn't happen here," Greenwood said. "I've got no warrant."

"I meant from a personal standpoint. As his uncle?"

"I can't afford the time away from here," Greenwood said.

"Not even to find the men who killed your nephew?" Clint asked.

"I have responsibilities here, Adams—"

"Never mind," Clint said.

"Sorry you came here for nothin'."

"Oh," Clint said, "I didn't come for nothing."

He left the office without explaining.

Clint put Roscoe Bookbinder's guns on the gunsmith's desk.

"Hey, I remember these," the man said.

"Good," Clint said. "I was hoping you would."

"Sure, I took those pearl handles off."

"Do you still have them?"

The man frowned. "Am I supposed to still have them?"

"Look, relax," Clint said. "If you sold them, or used them—"

"No, no," the gunsmith said. "I still have them. What do you want me to do?"

"Put 'em back," Clint said.

"Back on these guns?"

"Yes."

The man scratched his head.

"Don't worry," Clint said. "I'll pay for them."

The man brightened, grabbed the guns, and said, "Right away."

Clint walked out of the man's shop with the pearl-handled pistols in his hands. He hung them over his saddle, and started his search for Zack Foley and his four compadres . . .

They weren't hard to find. As he stared at them from across the room, he was surprised that they had all stayed together. Then again, when five men have to get together to kill one, they can't be men who feel very secure when they're alone. They were probably firm believers that there was safety in numbers.

He was there to prove them wrong.

FORTY-THREE

Clint put the rest of the beer down on the bar and walked over to the table of five men. They were so busy laughing and slapping one another on the back that they didn't notice him standing there. When they did, four of them didn't recognize him, but the fifth—Zack—looked startled.

"Hey, uh—" he said, but Clint cut him off.

"You didn't think you'd get away with it, did you, Zack?" he asked. "Riding in and shooting the kid to pieces like that?"

"Who is this guy, Zack?" one of the men asked.

"Who're you?" Clint asked.

"Eric Stride," the man said, standing up. "What's it to ya?"

"My name's Clint Adams."

Stride stared at him, then sat back down. The other men at the table looked nervous.

"You all thought you got away with it, but you haven't," Clint said.

Zack looked at Clint, then at the twin rig he was wearing, with pearl-handled guns.

"That's right," Clint said. "I'm wearing the kid's guns. It's time to pay."

"Hey, mister," one of the other men said, "we don't know nothin'—"

"Yeah, yeah, I know," Clint said. "You don't know nothing about killing no kid."

"Never mind," Zack said to his friends. "We got him outnumbered five to one."

"That's right," Clint said, "just like Roscoe Book-binder. Five to one. Come on, fill me full of lead."

Clint backed up and suddenly there was a flurry of movement as patrons scattered to get out of the way of flying lead. The bartender dropped down behind the bar.

"Stand up!" Clint shouted.

"Come on, stand up," Zack said to the others, getting to his feet. "I ain't backin' down again. He can't take all of us."

Everybody in the room was crouching down or trying to hide behind something, but also didn't want to miss anything.

Slowly, the other men at the table stood up. A couple of them wiped their hands on their thighs.

"It don't matter if you got that kid's fancy guns," Zack said. "You can't outdraw all of us."

"I don't have to outdraw you, Zack," Clint said. "I just have to outshoot you."

"He's crazy," Randle said. "Let's walk out of here."

"Nobody walks," Clint said. "If any of you walk out of here, it will mean I'm dead."

"Then die, damn you," Zack said, and went for his gun.

Clint drew with both hands. The five men rushed their shots and mostly broke glass and bottles on the bar behind Clint. He, on the other hand, very methodically put a bullet into each man, then picked out the ones he thought needed a second bullet and delivered those. Something tugged at his right shirtsleeve, but that was the closest a bullet came to hitting him.

When it was all over, it was deathly quiet in the room. Until somebody moved a chair, dragging it over the floor. Then others started to move, coming forward to look down at the five dead men.

"I don't believe it," somebody said.

"Fastest thing I ever saw," another man said.

Clint removed the gun belt and slapped it down on the bar in front of the stunned bartender. He then walked out of the saloon, got on Eclipse, and rode out of Ellsworth, Kansas.

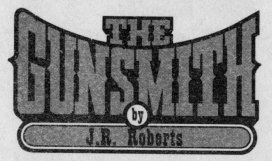

GIANT ACTION! GIANT ADVENTURE!

THE GUNSMITH

J.R. ROBERTS

penguin.com/actionwesterns